PRAISE FOR *TRUE*

"This book broke my heart and put it back together again. This isn't just about the culture of high-stakes, highly competitive youth sports; True is about how friendship grows into rivalry, the powerful conflict between ambition and image, and the responsibilities to family pitted against responsibility to the whims and desires of your own heart. I was rooting for True through every suspenseful and chaotic page; believe me, you will too."

—Charles Bock, bestselling author of *Alice & Oliver*

"I can't recall the last time I encountered a narrator as compelling as True. She is as strong as she is vulnerable and as talented as she is isolated and as single-minded as she is reckless. Have you ever wanted anything so badly that you broke bones for it? This is the story of that kind of want, the point at which drive and desire collude, commiserate, combust. And the prose. Karl Taro Greenfeld writes with a disarming, almost subversive intimacy that will own you from the very first page. I want this book in the hands of every reader I know. Yes. It's that good."

—Jill Alexander Essbaum, author of *New York Times* bestselling novel *Hausfrau*

"*True* is a dark and lively ode to the single-minded dedication required of greatness, a *Black Swan* on the pitch. I couldn't put it down."

—Amelia Gray, author of *Isadora* and *Gutshot: Stories*

"There's only one thing you can say after reading *True*: Karl Taro Greenfeld is one of the best writers around. Get ready. This book will destroy you."

—Scott McClanahan, author of *The Sarah Book*

"Greenfeld writes from the perspective of a young woman with ease and believability; there are no false notes here, not a single moment that I didn't feel completely invested in, and half in love with, True. *True* feels as if it were written in a dream, as if Greenfeld was only there to transcribe it, which is what every writer hopes to achieve in a novel."

—Mary Miller, author of *Big World, The Last Days of California*, and *Always Happy Hour*

"*True* held me in thrall as I followed its namesake narrator from girlhood to adulthood. With so many coming-of-age stories showcasing characters searching for themselves, True knows exactly who she is. It's the rest of her world—father, sister, coach, teammates, lovers—that expects more from her, that expects her to fall in line as countless girls and women before her have done. This is a heartbreaking, riveting tale of what it is to be yourself, no matter what."

—Lindsay Hunter, author of *Ugly Girls, Don't Kiss Me,* and *Eat Only When You're Hungry*

TRUE

ALSO BY KARL TARO GREENFELD

The Subprimes
Triburbia
NowTrends
Boy Alone
China Syndrome
Standard Deviations
Speed Tribes

TRUE

A NOVEL

KARL TARO GREENFELD

Little a

Published by Little A, New York
www.apub.com

ISBN-13: 9781542046831 (hardcover)
ISBN-10: 1542046831 (hardcover)

ISBN-13: 9781542046848 (paperback)
ISBN-10: 154204684X (paperback)

Cover design by Joan Wong

Printed in the United States of America

First edition

For Esmee

AUTHOR'S NOTE

This is a work of fiction about a character that exists within the highly competitive world of women's soccer. I have set important parts of the story in connection with the actual USA women's team active in the years 1997–2004 and have referenced players that are likely known to readers. I have used these players because they are important to the sport at the time depicted in the novel. Any dialogue or action attributed to these players in the novel is fictional.

PROLOGUE

2004

I call this the Argentine and African game, just as I call the game at University High School the Mexican and Salvadoran game, or the Sunday-morning game at Will Rogers the Italian game. The truth is, there's always a mix of nationalities, but there are universal types you become familiar with if you play pickup soccer in Los Angeles. There are tall, efficient Middle Europeans who seem to see every angle and will surprise you with sudden speed; there are finicky, injury- and argument-prone Italians on pencil-thin calves who are capable of making the ball vanish for hundredths of a second, only for it to reappear behind you; there are dreadlocked Jamaicans who play barefooted and in sunglasses but are so strong that their wake shakes you as they run past; stout Latinos who, no matter how old and unfit, will still gracefully slide tackle the ball from you; Africans who laugh while they dribble past you. There are Jews who wear yarmulkes while they play their surprisingly nimble game, former American college players who wear old fraternity T-shirts and never tire, Persians who have the latest soccer shoes and hiss at you when they want the ball, slightly too-old fathers who play alongside their slightly too-young sons. Which type am I? I am, of course, the girl.

I arrive alone on a hot, dry February day and park my white Toyota Celica, the same car I drove all through high school and college, gather my University of California at Miramar duffel with the Nike logo on one side, and take slow, careful steps on feet blistered and scarred, toenails cracked, some gone entirely, skin pink and bloody where keratin is stripped, third and fourth toes so often broken they're curled down, like talons, the whole mess bandaged, taped, wrapped. I wear a loose-fitting hoodie, black knee-length leggings, and acrylic outer shorts, and I take the descending stairs gingerly, trudge across the asphalt path, and come onto grass, late-afternoon sun still high, players already dressed and stretched, having a kickaround. I have a slightly pigeon-toed walk, not much air under my soles when I step, and I tend to watch my feet as I go. I am careful. I am already damaged.

Sometimes, there's another girl already there, and then I have to make a quick calculation: Do I befriend her, ignore her, try to intimidate her? What if she's better than I am? (Never happened.) If she's too pretty, that means she's there to watch, not to play. I hate myself for already knowing that and the implication: I am there to play, not to watch. So what does that make me?

When I first came out, the boys pretended not to notice or care, but there was the tacit assessment, in whatever language: not her, not on my team. Because the girl, usually, is the weaker player. It's a matter of physiology, lung capacity, tendon strength, foot length; there are a number of reasons why most males are better at soccer than most females, but let's start with two: size and speed. So if I'm new, I have to wait, to join a pickup side looking for a sixth or to be the body that evens out an odd match.

I'm not impressive in warm-ups; I don't do those ball tick-tacking tricks, juggling from left foot to right, from right knee to left, to head, to nape, and then back down to the feet. I can, if I like, but they strike me as vulgar and have nothing to do with loosening up for a match. I touch face to knee in old-school tibialis and flexor-muscle stretches, the kind children have been doing in physical education classes since before females were allowed to participate in physical education. I stand, crossing legs and bending forward, and then I run, frontward and then backward, around and around whatever pitch we're playing on, until I sweat.

I'm short and stocky with sturdy calves, thick thighs, wide haunches, small stomach that shows a four-pack of abdominals, small breasts smothered and made to look even flatter in a sports bra, surprisingly long neck, small face, weak chin, thin lips, a twice-broken nose dimpled by acne scars, always reddened by too much sun after I work off the sunscreen, wide blue eyes, narrow forehead showing a few horizontal wrinkles, and brown hair. Overall, the impression I give once I've kitted up in cleats and shin guards, and pulled my extra-large polyester shorts over my leggings, is of a pubescent male wrestler who's stepped outside the gym for the first time, hoping to try his luck at a new sport.

But once we play, I become me. I'm faster than I look—yes, I mean fast *for a girl*, but fast enough to play with boys—and I have a good feel for the ball: soft first touch, can pass with either foot, finish with either, and I will keep running, even chasing down loose balls, until you're on your back, cramped and puking. I've crossed players up so badly, with a feint right, a touch left, that they fall over, literally, as if I've drained their blood. I won't bore you with a litany of the beautiful moments I keep stored inside my head, but you get the idea. I can play with the boys.

BOOK I

1997

Chapter 1

Oh, the great strides we've made. I was in middle school when Congress passed the Equity in Athletics Disclosure Act, which put teeth into Title IX, and the colleges came looking for female athletes. If you played a team sport, or ran, or threw, or jumped, or swam, or did almost anything that boys also did, then every university in America needed you so that they could continue to field teams of boys who ran, or threw, or jumped, or swam.

I've been a soccer player since I could walk. My father kicked the ball around with me on our downward-sloping front yard, where for my entire life Spanish moss spread over the brick patio but never entirely covered it. There's video, likely taken by my mother, of me at eighteen months, running naked across the grass, kicking the ball forward. I can hear my parents cheering as I run. I chase the ball until it settles against my father's bare foot.

What strikes me, when I watch footage of myself at that age, is how I was in no way disappointing in my shape and form. From that baby running to kick that ball, you couldn't extrapolate my future boxiness, my—how else to put it?—unsinewyness, my thickness, my fire-hydrant-like lack of appeal. Now, I have a body that's functional; it's good for soccer, for kicking that ball, but that just isn't enough, is it? No matter how many soap and lotion advertisements celebrate the diversity of female bodies, I know, and you know, which are the most highly prized. It's the girl who comes to the game to watch, not to play.

I've played organized soccer since I was four years old. My father coached my first team before I qualified for traveling teams, Select teams, Tri-County teams, and the National Soccer Coaches Association of America regional teams; he took his turn dutifully driving me to distant soccer fields, spending his Sundays with four girls in his Volvo station wagon, driving ninety minutes to Anaheim or San Dimas for us to play a group of Mexican girls who looked like they were in their twenties.

He wasn't one of those fathers who shouted my name or barked commands while I played. He'd stand at the touchline, hands in his pockets, watching the game through his sunglasses, smoking a cigarette that he held behind his back between puffs, as if to hide it. A few yards away, sitting on the lawn, would be my sister, Pauline, twiddling blades of grass between her fingers, chewing a stick. When there were quartered oranges at halftime, she'd wander over, and my father would remove the peel from a few sections, and she would take her orange and return to her patch of grass, bobbing her head if she was in a good mood, or banging her head against the grass if she was angry. When she threw a tantrum, my father would take her back to the car so that I wouldn't be distracted during my game. But he didn't have to worry. Back then, nothing distracted me.

There were so many leagues, so many coaches with their practical black football boots and Irish or Italian or Spanish accents, each with his own theory on the best way to practice: full-squad scrimmage, no scrimmages, six a side, four a side, ball drills, off-ball drills, running five miles a day, no running, strengthening the core, weight training, eschewing weight training. We were told to eat lean protein, drink milk, avoid caffeine, cut out sugar. No carbs on game day, carbo-load the day before. Some of us were introduced to endocrine drugs, which were meant to accelerate female puberty—hormones that could rush a girl's growth spurt so that she'd grow into her body sooner. Coaches and colleges needed to know: Would she be short and stocky, the classic boxy shape of a great footballer (Maradona), or would she be long with flicking limbs, a two-legged spider (Beckenbauer)? Either would do, but the sooner a girl arrived at her shape, the better. They needed to know what they were working with.

I asked my father, "Will I be tall?" Mom was tall, or so he always reminded me. Would I have calves bulging with tendon and muscle, thighs thick as car tires, feet soft as white bread? At that age, all I wanted was a body for soccer, nothing else. I wanted to be fast, to win the ball, to have a good first touch, to finish. Nothing else mattered. This, I learned, wasn't the case with the other girls.

The only bat mitzvahs I was invited to were my teammates'—Gwen's, Lorena's—and when I arrived at their parties, I was surprised to find how they'd made themselves over: a gown of some shimmery material, hair blown out, nails painted. Even my closest friend on the team, Alexis, turned from a grass-stained grade horse into some kind of burnished all-American colt, all legs and long skinny arms and curly blond hair. I saw it as a kind of betrayal, but if I'd just followed their line of sight, to where the boys were standing, it would have made quick sense.

Those other versions of themselves, the girls getting dirty on the pitch, were not their real selves. This—this girl in a light-blue dress, this girl wearing makeup to cover up acne and bruises—this was the real self.

The girls were all becoming real girls, and I was becoming me.

Soccer, at least back then, started with an appraisal of your genealogy. Latinas, despite their cultural *fútbol* heritage, were never given the benefit of the doubt. But a European accent meant you would always get a game. If you were African American, then the blacker, the better.

Africans can play. White girls always had to prove it. But we had a core group, seven of us, who had at that point already been proving it to each other for half a decade in Tri-County and Select. By the time we were in seventh grade, our school team, the Patriots, was the least important soccer team we played on. Our coach, a physical education teacher who knew less about the game than we did, rolled out a ball three afternoons a week, and we girls took it from there. Quickly, we determined our best eleven: our group of seven white girls, plus three Mexican girls and the black keeper. The Persians we ran off, and the Salvadorans and Guatemalans were told they could ride the bench. That was our middle school team, and we advanced all the way to the city finals, losing to a team of Chinese girls from Monterey Park who were even faster and meaner than we were. Alexis, Tri-County and Select MVP, was the best girl on our team, and I was the second best. Or was it the other way around? It didn't really matter. Our talent on the pitch somehow bound us together. I became so used to her position on the field—to my left and slightly forward of me—that when she wasn't there, I felt it like a missing tooth. When we rode to regional games together, long hours in the back seats of parents' cars, I even sat with her to my left.

As the core seven soccer girls bonded—on the Tri-County team, the Select team, then the NSCAA regional team—I came into my own. And for a bright season, while my father was still working with Pauline himself, while specialists from Loyola Marymount were still at our house most afternoons, and when incremental gains looked sustainable and additive—Pauline wiped herself, Pauline said "drink," Pauline pointed to a picture of a cookie to indicate her desire—I could convince myself that, though we were shorthanded, we were still a family of sorts, a winning team.

Around this time, my father discovered the upstairs room at Hops—one of the only establishments with a full liquor license in Pacific Point—where a few local fathers gathered and watched sports and played cards. At first, it was a place he stopped by on his way back from his office, a small, file cabinet–crammed room behind a smoked glass window with the name of his financial-advisory service stenciled in black. These were the last years of his practice, before the small punter switched to online brokerage accounts and my father's entire profession—middling quality, midrange investment advice for the middle class—became superannuated by algorithms and seven-dollar trades.

He was among the first financial advisers in Pacific Point to have a Quotron machine, and during his peak years, dentists and doctors and waiters came by his office for a quote. Micron. Sundancer Oil. EF Hutton. Global Crossing. Companies long since merged, collapsed, busted. Back when trades were denominated in sixteenths. But here's how quaint his business was: one of his competitive advantages was a direct line to floor specialists on the Pacific Exchange, a market that itself ceased to exist in 2001. I didn't know it, but by the time I finished middle school, my dad was thinking of big next steps: What could he possibly do with the rest of his life that would support his family?

Immersed in my soccer leagues, I was distracted enough to maintain hope that Pauline, through a combination of behavioral therapy and an act of God, would become a normal sister. Whenever I felt that creeping suspicion that our family was vexed, that Pauline would always be profoundly autistic, I would seek out a game. I would play soccer. It saves me.

The same seven of us attended Pacific Point, the public high school, and played for the Sea Lionesses, as the girls' teams were known. We finally had a real soccer coach, who shut us down when we tried to exclude the other girls, telling us that if we wanted to win, we had to put the best eleven out there, which meant all seven of us, of course, but also another four chosen by the coach—not us.

As close as the seven of us were on the pitch, our deltas had widened since those bat mitzvahs. When my teammates weren't playing, they dressed like real girls. I wore sweats every day. At first, during freshman year, there were a few tentative attempts to mainstream me into better outfits: fitted jeans, strappy evening tops, camouflage hoodies. Because I didn't have a mom, and my father wasn't inclined to investigate teen fashion, I was left to dress myself from my friends' castoffs. But I just wasn't built like the other girls. Alexis's mother drove us to the mall, and Alexis led me in and out of PacSun and Roxy, ending up with two bags for herself and nothing for me.

While the other girls were lengthening and budding and swelling in the predictable ways and in the right spots, I was just sort of hardening. I had muscles in places where the other girls didn't even have places. On the pitch, you couldn't knock me off the ball; I could free myself with an elbow the official would never see. But put me in a pair of pegged jeans, and it was too much muscle and meat shoved into sausage skins.

My teammates were kind—or, no, they weren't kind, but they weren't as cruel to me as we were to everyone else. Freshman season into sophomore, they gave me some sort of exemption, allowing me to sit with them at lunch, where we had the picnic table with the hard plastic top and the molded tubular steel frame next to the planter—a desirable spot. Alexis had emerged as the team leader and top girl in our clique, and she always saved a seat for me at the table, to her right. Maybe this was force of habit, the middle two of a 3-3-2-2 formation, or maybe it was that we always respected each other; and back then, we even liked each other. Sometimes, I would ride home with Alexis after school, and sometimes, I would do homework with short-haired, red-cheeked Lorena, our right back. But as for the rest of my teammates, I always wondered if they were prorating their sympathy based on the fact that I only had a dad and a profoundly autistic sister. They wanted to help me be more like them, though it was clear, for whatever reasons—maybe because I only had a dad, maybe because of Pauline, but maybe, really, just because of me—I could never be that much like them.

I was bringing down the group average, in terms of looks, style, cuteness, desirability, and all the other matrices so important to high school girls. But I was valuable. I contributed on the pitch to 12-2-2 and 13-1-2 seasons, and in tenth grade, I scored nine goals in the season and made the All City team. I was on my way to making the Diadora All-American first team—Alexis did—and having my photo in *Parade* magazine that year—Alexis did—but I picked up a red card and a two-game suspension in our sixth game when I punched a Ukrainian girl from Fairfax in the mouth.

After practices—showered and changed, fresh deodorant applied, dirty socks, sports bras, shorts in a pile at our feet—it felt, for a few minutes, like we were all equal. All of us in our sweats and slides, hair wet from the shower, carrying our duffels full of dirty kit and shoes to our cars. For an instant, it felt as though we were ten again, just wrapping up Tri-County practice at Rancho, and Alexis and I were walking together to the little snack shop to buy Powerade. But by eleventh grade, we didn't rush out to our parents' cars; instead, in ones or twos, we got into our own cars and then backed out and exited the hillside parking lot of Pacific Point High School. From the locker room, I had exactly twenty minutes to get to Pauline's day care program at a Methodist church in Santa Monica, or Noriko, the Japanese lady who ran the program, would call my father, angry at waiting the additional time, saying she would put Pauline into a taxi like she did with the other kids.

Almost three years my junior and my opposite in nearly every way, Pauline was beautiful, slender, and slow, while I was plain, thick, and fast. I walked at eight months; it took Pauline two and a half years. She was toilet trained at three, never learned to swim, and still couldn't ride a bike at fourteen. Maybe my looks were the price I paid for my gifts—speed, strength, agility, toughness. Wasn't that why college coaches were coming to watch me? Why I received letters every day from Division

I, II, and III soccer programs, many of which were just starting to fill the female rosters so they wouldn't have to forfeit a male soccer season? I had a box full of letters, and wasn't that proof that I had a gift? But I had to work for it, practice, forswear alcohol (not that I drank), forswear weed (not that I smoked), eschew fatty foods, and stuff myself with lean protein, while Pauline—excuse me for calling her a nitwit, but that's what she was—didn't have to do a thing.

Her eyes were wide and almond shaped (and so dumb), and her hair was raven black and naturally lustrous; her narrow nose descended to an outward bow like the flourish ending a cursive letter, her lips were full, and her jaw made a soft U-shaped chin. Everyone who saw her noted first that she was a pretty girl. When my father used to take us to the supermarket and Pauline was still small enough to ride in the shopping cart, strangers would stop us to tell us how beautiful she was. Those eyes, even then, were gigantic, giving her face an anime quality, as if she were too beautiful for this shaky handheld camera of a world that we lived in and existed in some other Technicolor realm.

No one commented on my looks.

I didn't know it, or I didn't *know it* know it, but we had gone from being a perfect family (dad, daughter, mom) to being an oddball family (dad, daughter, beautiful fucked-up baby, and no mom). But I had soccer. As early as my preschool years, the teachers told my father that I had some aptitude—I could run with the boys, even beat them at their games—and they suggested I sign up for biddy league. And as soon as I stepped on those pitches, even those diminutive small-goal little-kid fields, I forgot everything. I became someone else, and there was nothing strange about me, because there I fucking fit right in.

Chapter 2

Statistically, the absolute worst thing that can happen to a daughter is to lose her mother. It makes a girl half as likely to finish high school, a quarter as likely to complete college, and twice as likely to become drug dependent. She is at higher risk of teen pregnancy, of teen alcoholism, and even of being sexually molested, in part because there is no mother to keep the monsters of the world at bay. So losing our mother was a disaster for me, but for Pauline, who never had a mother, whose mother—our mother—died during her birth of a sudden aneurysm, it should have been an even crueler set of odds. Yet strangely—and here the statistics become murky—daughters who never had a mother actually perform better by all those societal metrics than daughters who had a mother and then lost her. So statistically, I was the unlucky one and not Pauline, who put up such a struggle coming out that our poor mother hemorrhaged to death from an aneurysm in just eight minutes, doctors reluctant to trephine her skull during the birth lest she lose the child.

Well, she didn't lose the child. We lost a mother.

But I could never tell that to Pauline, who was sitting in a sandbox, floodwater jeans hiked up over mismatched socks, T-shirt with collar chewed off, hair knotty.

"B-b-b-b-b-b," she said, a string of gibberish consonants, before she settled on "T-t-t-t-t-t"—the first consonant of my name, Trudy. She nodded her head, and nodded again. There was the nodding, the rocking, the shaking of her head, the lifting of her arm, the turning of her hand. She had an endless assortment of these tics, but she also smiled. And when she saw me, she always smiled. "T-t-t-t-t-t—"

"Get up," I told her. "Pauline, get up."

"G-g-g-g-g-g-go," she said.

"Go home. We go home."

She stood. I brushed the damp sand from her jeans, checked if she'd wet herself, and counted myself lucky when I felt a dry bum through her pants.

Noriko came out, nodded when she saw me, and then, as if recalling something, went back inside. While I strapped Pauline into the back seat of the Celica, Noriko returned with a manila envelope.

We drove, and I talked to Pauline, told her about my day, practice, the team. I was in high school. I hated high school. Or I hated the school part of high school. Soccer I loved. And I kept my B average so I could stay eligible for the team. English was easy enough. *To Kill a Mockingbird*, *The Catcher in the Rye*, and *Native Son* went down quickly and were regurgitated into essays: topic sentence, quote, expository sentence, quote, concluding sentence. There was my paragraph. Five of those and I had an essay. But AP Chemistry was a dark mystery. I wasn't a great student, but I was a fast reader and quick writer. And I was quiet, could sit through class, head down, eyes squinted at the laws of thermodynamics or the principles of oxidation and reduction. It was like eating the Ryvita bread that soccer coaches sometimes told us was a better carb than white bread: dull, flavorless, good for us.

Pauline, who was forever shut out of mainstream life, of high school, was always intensely curious about my school. There was talk, years before, of Pauline mainstreaming into a regular school, but even with heavy antipsychotics and sedatives, she could never make it. I knew as soon as my father returned from a progress-report meeting at Pauline's program: she would never walk down the halls of a normal middle school. She still had accidents where she shit herself. I knew you couldn't shit yourself at school, no matter how progressive the school community.

But she liked hearing my stories of school, of my schedule, which I repeated to her every day and she forgot every day.

"AP Chem, Spanish 2, AP Lang, Honors History, Cooking, soccer."

"A-a-a-a-a-a P K-k-k-k-k." She tried to say it.

"Chemistry."

"K-k-k-k-k-kem-m-m-m-m," she said.

"Chemistry."

I told her I still sat with the other girls from the team at lunch, at the picnic table next to the planter, where the popular kids sat.

But I hadn't sat with my teammates since sophomore year. As a junior, I ate lunch by myself, sometimes in the soccer coach's office, or if he was busy, I sat against the brick wall outside his office and ate my sliced lean chicken breasts.

I didn't tell Pauline, but the girls on the team grew past me, or grew past putting up with me. There were boys, gangly, gap-toothed, flattering boys, who flocked around my teammates and huddled with them in whispered conversations. Nobody asked me to sit elsewhere; it was a decision I made, to withdraw rather than be ignored.

The same girls, the seven of us—Alexis, Gwen, Tori, Claire, Nicky, Lorena, and I—had played together for close to a decade by then. We'd literally tasted each other's blood in on-the-field collisions, but it turned out we weren't friends. Or that I didn't know how to be a friend.

But I told Pauline that I sat with the same girls, the girls she remembered from tagging along to Tri-County, made her believe that I was a typical high school girl, that I was the normal one, that everything was working out for me, that I had friends and was popular and life was easy for me. It was my duty to have the normal life, since Pauline had a resolute hold on abnormal. So I pretended, for her sake, for everyone's sake.

It's what Pauline wanted to hear—at least I thought it was, but I didn't know that for sure.

I didn't know what went on in her mind. She was self-absorbed, solipsistic—the symptoms of the deeply autistic, the dagger edge of the spectrum. Her IQ had been described as untestable, which meant she was below what used to be called mentally retarded. She seldom evinced much curiosity and rarely asked a question, but when she did, it was always directed toward me, and always about school, the normal school, another normal thing among the countless normal things she would never be able to do.

Pacific Point hunkered on palisades over the Coast Highway, the foamy Pacific beyond, one- and two-story ranch and Spanish-style houses strung on canyon roads, green front lawns going brown, sprinklers hissing, darkness spreading like ill will from east to west, where the sun dropped into the ocean, an orange quarter into a video game slot. Play and turn the world black.

Pauline sat belted in the back seat. She wasn't allowed to sit in front, where she could grab the wheel or throw the transmission. It was safer with her in back, diagonal from me—the last defender in a 3-3-2-2—though this also made it easier for her to remove her shoes and toss them out the window, so I put the windows on child lock. On that particular day, Pauline was pleased to see me, so she was sitting still, repeating over and over, "B-b-b-b-b-broken, b-b-b-b-b-broken."

"It's a red light," I told her. "It's not broken."

"B-b-b-b-b-b."

The light turned, and we went up the winding streets, past the soccer field, past my old elementary school, to park in the flat driveway where grass grew in the cracks in the pavement. I opened the door, walked around the car, and let Pauline out, and she ran onto the

Spanish-moss lawn and sat down, grabbing a handful of grass, lifting it to her nose as if smelling it. Then she started rocking, twiddling the blades between thumb and forefinger. She would have sat there for hours if I'd let her.

An older gentleman walking a dog pretended not to notice anything.

"Come on," I told her, walking toward the front door, hoping Pauline would follow.

"What's up, True?"

I turned. Alexis was driving her silver BMW Touring wagon, leaning across Brendan, her boyfriend, a spiker for the volleyball team, with long blond hair, a gap in his teeth, and sharp, lupine eyes. He was cruelly beautiful, the male version of Alexis. Alexis had blown out her right knee before arthroscopic surgery made recovery for a lithe and athletic sixteen-year-old pro forma, back when injuries like this could be career ending. That had been the saddest day of my soccer career up to that point. It could have ended the career of a less formidable competitor than Alexis. It had been a simple turn, all her weight on her right knee, a move she had made dozens of times every day of her soccer life, but this time, in an intra-squad scrimmage, her knee had bowed. The anterior cruciate ligament was torn—a paper cut–sized gap, but still severed. Before her knee injury, the ball had seemed glued to her foot; it took a gang of Chinese girls to rob her, and she could turn and fire with either foot in a space the size of a phone booth. (Who killed Upland Rangers in the NSCAA semifinals? It was Alexis, in their pantry, with a soccer ball.) But then came her injury. She was the first of us—of the seven who dominated West Los Angeles youth soccer for the better part of a decade—to fall. She'd been reduced to playing backup minutes, at least until her knee returned to full strength, but she remained as fiercesomely beautiful as ever, modeling blouses and dresses for a boutique in Santa Monica, her position at the head of our soccer clique secured by her looks as much as her talent. She worked zealously in the swimming pool, in the weight room. She swore that after her rehab, she'd be even quicker than she was before her injury.

I never doubted her.

I stood between my car and my sister, my Umbro soccer duffel on my left shoulder, my school backpack on my other. I stared at Brendan and Alexis. He was so beautiful. She was so beautiful. Pauline was so beautiful.

"What's going on?" shouted Alexis.

I pointed to my sister. Pauline rocked back and forth.

"Hey, Paul!"

Pauline, who'd known Alexis since we'd played small-goal biddy soccer together, looked up at Alexis and smiled.

"*That's* Trudy's sister?" I heard Brendan say. "Damn, True has a hot sister!"

"Don't be a dick, Brendan," Alexis said. "You don't talk about True's sister."

I couldn't hear the conversation that followed, but it looked like Alexis was lecturing Brendan. Brendan stared down at his hands, and then up at Pauline, and then back at his hands.

"Sorry, True, he's an idiot," Alexis said. She shifted her gaze to Pauline. "Bye, Paul." They drove off.

Pauline smiled.

"D-d-d-d-d-d-d," she said, asking for our father.

Chapter 3

Statistically, the surviving husband of a wife who dies in childbirth is more likely to end up incarcerated; to be on public assistance; to abuse alcohol, drugs, and tobacco; to have his children become wards of the state; and to live a shorter life span than those who never married, those who divorced, and, of course, those whose wives didn't pass away.

My father didn't know what to do with Pauline. By the time she was a year old, it was apparent she wouldn't follow the developmentally typical path of her older sister. I'd done the usual—playgroups, preschool, and Reading with Mom events at the local library, only with my dad. My father doted on me, made up stories for me, burned through books with me. But soon, very soon, too soon, his attention shifted. He still drove me to my Tri-County games, took his turn in the parental carpool, and made sure I had new boots and a new kit, but then there she was: the beautiful, troubled Pauline, who couldn't do anything on schedule—sit up, crawl, walk. She missed every mark on that growth-and-progress chart the doctor gave my father with stunning regularity.

He did everything he could, enrolling Pauline in the best programs he could find and securing her Regional Center funding—government money allocated to autistic children according to the Individuals with Disabilities Education Act. He learned all the acronyms: IDEA, FAPE, ADA, ABA. He'd arranged for a comprehensive evaluation for an individualized family service plan (IFSP) so that Pauline could receive an appropriate early intervention at thirty months, and he'd spent so much of my childhood seated at a table, administering applied behavior analysis (ABA), the operant conditioning, the laborious attempt to train my sister with positive reinforcements for correct behaviors.

Pauline, as soon as she could walk, was a dervish of activity, rocking, shaking her head, twiddling string or rubber bands between her fingers, and it was viewed as a matter of some urgency, by the doctors and the specialists who saw Pauline, that she be compelled to sit in one place long enough to actually learn something. The goal—always dangled like this elusive prize my family could win only if my father worked hard enough, if we all worked hard enough, hired specialists, speech therapists, physical therapists, counselors, psychiatrists, paid for the right medications, somehow secured spots in the right schools, fed Pauline the right diets, if we built a life totally devoted in every way to Pauline—was to mainstream her into a normal school, which, as I said, was obviously never going to happen. In schools, you sat at a desk and you worked, neither of which Pauline looked likely to ever do.

But my father would sit across a table from her in her room, M&M's next to him in a cup, and urge Pauline to sit, to sit, to sit. And it was a supreme act of effort on her part to stop rocking and sit still, for five seconds, six, seven, to earn that little piece of candy.

I believed that my father would somehow fix Pauline through this intensive obedience school–style regimen. My father, his brow furrowing as he read up on the subject, was inspired by the reports that as many as 50 percent—no, 70 percent; no, 75 percent!—of kids diagnosed with autism who received intense early intervention recovered and were performing at 75 percent of grade level by the time they were high school age. But Pauline, who was also diagnosed with an intellectual disability, was at the lower end of the spectrum, at the murky dark end where those statistics didn't apply, where, it turns out, nobody was even bothering to do studies to come up with any statistics. Because those kids were generally untestable.

We didn't know. We were told to believe. We trekked to Pauline's specialists and to her early-intervention program at Loyola Marymount University, and we met other children just a few years older than Pauline who were practically normal. They were reading. They were verbal! Pretty soon, I assumed, my sister would be talking. She would be, well, like a sister. But until then, how good would I have to be to offset how bad my sister was? I pushed myself. Hard. It wasn't good enough to be good; I had to be the best.

Soon my father realized that Pauline wasn't progressing as quickly as those other autistic children had, those early-intervention success stories who were doing grade-level work by the time they were teens. But he kept it to himself.

Sometimes I try to remember what life was like before Pauline. We have never been a family that keeps framed photos in our living room—Pauline would toss them to the floor in a tantrum, just as she regularly turns over our coffee table and end tables. But I've seen photos of my father when he was young: narrow forehead, squinting blue eyes, bushy blond mustache, a barrel chest, thick legs. In one picture, he's standing next to a lifeguard tower in Santa Monica with my mother, Tonjua, the genetic source of Pauline's fine attributes, beside him, the two of them like a sheriff and the best-looking dame in the saloon. You can't see a dash of sadness about them, because the future must have looked as uncloudy as those Santa Monica skies.

My dad was an avid sailor, winning third place in Finn class in the state championships during a rough-water weekend off Santa Cruz, conditions in which a high school kid from an inland city like Sacramento, a charity case at Folsom Lake Yacht Club, was supposed to finish DFL. He was so comfortable on the water, so sure of his footing, his weight on the boat, the edge, the jib, the telltales. He could take a rotting ketch in dead calm and find gust and six knots. Dad lacked the scratch to keep a hull in the water on the regular. He hauled a Hobie Cat 18 down to the Marina del Ray boat launch on a trailer every weekend and sailed as far as Catalina or down to China Beach or up to Port Hueneme. (He never paid the registration fees.) One of my first memories is of sailing with him and my mom. I'm strapped to his chest in a front-facing pack as he's tacking the boat into a dock in Catalina and then swinging across the main mast to the gangway, the handrails wreathed in spiderweb. After Pauline arrived, I don't think the boat went into the water again. It sat in the driveway until finally he sold it through an ad in the *Recycler*, a package deal with the trailer without working brake lights. But he never stopped loving sailing, and years later, he still talked about taking it up again, renting a Hobie Mirage, and feeling the spit and spray in his face. "I'll teach you, True. I'll teach you."

That's why he kept the life vests. And he never lost the rope calluses.

He stored his dreams in the garage. Those life vests, the photos, the typewriter . . . my dad was going to be a writer, a novelist, a screenwriter, and when he met my mom, she was going to become an actress. With his brains and her beauty, the world should have been theirs. I mean, statistically, aren't physically attractive people more likely to be happy than the rest of us? I'm not in a position to judge his aptitude as a writer, but I did read the pile of manuscript pages he'd buried away in the garage.

His novel is a story about a boy who loves sailing but gives up the sport to go to an inland college. From his descriptions of being at sea, of tacking a small cutter by himself off the California coast, of seals and sea lions, of sailfish and stingrays, of diving for sea urchins and abalones, it's easy to see how he loved that one thing in the same way that I love soccer, that he felt like himself only when he was at sea. And going inland, away from the ocean, it nearly kills him. His book seemed to be about seeing how his life wouldn't work out before it had even not worked out.

But then, in his novel, he returns to his coastal village. He finds a beautiful girl with long black hair, like my mom. They settle in their little town, in a little one-story house, and they have a daughter. She's named Barbara, but they nickname her Bullet, because of her speed.

And the three of them—the mother, father, and daughter—go out to sea together. They swim in little coves, Bullet conks her first fish, a striped sea bass, and the story sort of loses steam there. Because what is there to say about happy people?

I read his manuscript while I was recovering from my first broken nose, a memento from an NSCAA game against Calabasas Elite when I was thirteen. I was embarrassed by the sex scenes in the book.

But my dad never did finish that novel, and before I was born, he passed the Series 7 exam and became a financial adviser. He gave up on becoming a writer and worked primarily with a few of his friends who'd gone on to some success in show business—directors, an actor or two. During my childhood, some of my dad's more famous colleagues would periodically turn up at our house, an actor I recognized from a Farrelly brothers movie or a producer on a sitcom I had seen. But as the years passed, the gap between my dad and his friends broadened, and once his own famously lovely wife passed away, the rich and glamorously successful no longer stopped by; it turned out that she was our family's most powerful attraction all along.

That morning when Mom died, when Pauline was born, was the fulcrum. Those who knew my parents and had perhaps already purchased flowers and balloons, expecting us to be expecting, must have marked this as the turning point for my father, from lucky and handsome to unlucky and untalented. We swung from impending joy to sudden tragedy.

I was two and a half when Pauline was born. I was waiting at home with a babysitter, who'd allowed me to eat all the peanut M&M's I'd wanted the night before, when my father drove my mother to the hospital. I was standing at the front door when my father came in, holding my sister, and I looked past him to find my mother, as if she should have been back there somewhere, but she wasn't there. That's all I remember of the birth and death.

I have photos of my mother standing with me on her hip, a pair of cat-eye sunglasses on her face, her long black hair falling in luxuriant waves, like a pair of giant, vertical tildes framing her face. A close-up of her leaning over my crib, her vast black eyes almost but not quite too large for her face, gazing at the camera, my face toward hers instead of the camera.

Pauline has no recollection, no idea of our mother. She has our mother's looks, her eyes, her hair, but no memory of the person who gave them to her. Are her looks a blessing or a curse? Or are they her tragic flaw? Hester Prynne's passion. Veronica Sawyer's apathy. My sister's beauty.

Without my mother around, my father tried to teach me through books, always insisting that I read, shoving old editions of *White Fang* or *Treasure Island* at me—books with beveled cloth covers he bought for a quarter from the library bargain bin. I read them dutifully, then compulsively, tunneling into stories for the escape. And then I turned sixteen and just stopped. I was done with reading.

I was a soccer player first and a sister second. Or maybe it was the other way around.

Chapter 4

My father stood at the front door, a long, dark figure haloed in yellow porch light. "Pauline, get up," he said.

I handed my father the envelope from the day care center, filed past him into the house, and then shoved my shin guards, sports bras, leggings, tights, jerseys, and socks into the washing machine next to the kitchen, poured in soap, and started the Kenmore.

Once Pauline was in the house, he told me to watch her for a few minutes. He was going to Hops, the Chinese restaurant, and said he'd bring back sweet-and-sour pork, rice, chow mein, and shrimp. "Okay," I said. I didn't call bullshit. I didn't tell him that yes, I knew he was going to the Chinese restaurant, but that he was going to the upstairs room to play hold 'em or pai gow with Fernando and Carlos, the Mexican owners who'd taken over the joint from the founding Chinese fellow, Hop, a decade ago.

I told him to leave me twenty dollars. He handed me the bill. I'd buy two pounds of chicken breast for me, and white bread and bologna for Pauline. It would mean putting Pauline back into the car, driving to Hughes, and taking her into the store, where she'd draw everyone's attention, first for her looks, then for her behavior, while I quickly gathered up our shopping.

It was frustrating to indulge my father's gambling addiction, particularly since it was an addiction he'd had to work for, heading out most nights to Hops, playing cards with a motley assortment of husbands, bachelors, tradesmen, salesmen, and waiters on their breaks. First it was card games, two-four or three-six hold 'em, pai gow if there were enough players. Then it was in-season betting cards: football, basketball, baseball, European soccer. But try as he did, my father wasn't a degenerate gambler. He played within his means—a few dry spells excepted when I didn't have chicken money—but he didn't gamble the mortgage, or if he did, he won it back before I knew about it. There were other guys up at Hops who were destined for Gamblers Anonymous, like the fisherman who owed every mahi-mahi he conked to Fernando and Carlos for the rest of the decade, probably. But he still showed up, feet in flip-flops, his tabby cat trailing behind him into the smoky room.

I packed Pauline into the car, we got our groceries, and when we got home, I unpacked Pauline and the groceries. But instead of fixing our food, I found the unopened letter from Pauline's day care center sitting on the kitchen counter. I opened it. We were $1,570 behind in payments, the missed months adding up to almost a year, and Regional Center had already put in what it was going to put in. The day care center wanted $200 that week, or Pauline was out. So I loaded Pauline into the car, and we drove down to Hops. I parked in the back and told Pauline to wait in the car. I didn't want to subject her to a room full of leering men.

"M-m-m-m-m-m-m-m-m-m."

My father was sitting in front of a folded hand, ice water in a glass next to the cards, the fisherman across from him, the usual suckers seated around them. The cat, as if sensing an opportunity, had already found my legs and was rubbing against me.

"What's up, True?" my father asked.

I whispered in his ear about the day care center, how I had given him the letter at home but he had never opened it.

He took five twenties from the table and handed them to me. That's all the day care center would get.

But I needed more.

I needed to make a tape of me playing soccer to send to the Under-17 Olympic Development Program camp. My teammates already had two spots, and my coach said he could get my tape in front of Tony, the national women's team coach who would select the Olympic Development rosters.

I reached over and grabbed another eighty dollars from the table. "For me," I told my dad, my finger in his face.

"Hey, hey." He put his hands up, showing his fellow card players that he had no choice but to go along with the robbery.

This won sympathy around the table, and a few players tossed tens or twenties my way—pounds of chicken breasts, weeks of day care, a tape for my future, a bounty. I had been relying on the kindness of my teammates' parents for years, as they paid my way to our Select and NSCAA teams, my value as a player earning my plane tickets and travel trips. As long as I could help their daughters win—and perhaps attract the attention of Division I coaches—then it was worth paying my freight. At some point, that calculation would no longer add up, as the attention I was drawing away from their own offspring would cancel out my contributions to a winning team. I would have to pay my own way. Soon.

When I returned to the car, Pauline was still sitting there, waiting.

At home, I ran her bath, undressed her, told her to sit down and pee, wiped her, and then eased her into the tub. Pauline was long and slender, her legs unmarred and unscarred, unshaven, her ankles delicate. She had black pubic hair, thick and bushy; slender hips; a narrow waist; shapely but small breasts; and a long, elegant neck, her frame that of a supermodel shrunken down to a fourteen-year-old. I held her feet, so finely formed, and inspected her toenails. They'd do for now. Cutting Pauline's toenails was harrowing. She squirmed. She howled. I sometimes cut too close, drawing blood, which terrified Pauline—and me.

The whole operation was so exhausting that I occasionally let her nails grow until they were curled. They weren't there yet.

"D-d-d-d-d-d-d-d-d-d."

"Daddy's at the Chinese restaurant," I told her. I let her soak.

In the kitchen, I ripped open chicken breast packages, doused the meat in soy sauce, catsup, honey, barbecue sauce, garlic, anything else I could find, and let the meat marinate. I'd broil it all in the oven at four hundred degrees and eat it for breakfast, lunch, and dinner the next day.

I pulled Pauline out of the tub, dried her, and slipped her into a pair of high-waisted bloomers and a T-shirt. I gambled that she wouldn't wet her bed.

Chapter 5

Every Tuesday of junior year, we ran hummingbirds. Coach Drixler would drop the team off at the bottom of the Latigo Canyon, tell us to run up the curving mountain road, and then wait thirty-five minutes before driving up and gathering us, the slowest first and the fastest last. If you were the last to be collected, you got out of two suicide drills. Coach Drixler called the runs "hummingbirds" because our hearts were supposed to be flapping through our chests from working so hard.

I was usually 150 yards ahead of the nearest girl.

My tape, when we made it, cut together video footage of me scoring goals, making good passes, taking penalty kicks, firing worm burners, and making clean tackles and smart, surprising runs. It showed a girl who stood surprisingly tall on the pitch. For a small player, compact, close to the ground, with a low center of gravity, I used every inch of my height, always surveying the field. Other players tended to ball watch, but I had developed the habit of looking at other players instead of the ball, noting where they were and where the open space was. The ball is always the easiest thing on the field to find, the fastest object on the pitch. But open space is the hardest to find, because the eye doesn't naturally search for nothing. I had a knack for finding the emptiness. And once I had the ball, I already knew where I was going with it, because I'd already made that first touch, in my head at least.

On the tape, I looked like I was a prairie dog, my head popping up and then down, up and then down, and my teammates, even those with good speed and fine touches, were looking at their feet.

But more than anything else, what I looked like on that tape was in control, in my element; my movement was efficient, my runs had a purpose, and my passes had velocity and pace and direction. I was balanced; my weight always seemed perfectly settled on both my feet, even when my stride was uneven. Because I didn't need my arms to keep my balance, even at pace, I could squeeze into gaps that other players couldn't even see. Their outstretched arms kept them vertical, but I could slide sideways into a space after releasing the ball. I looked like I belonged on that pitch.

Coach Drixler sent my tape to the Olympic Development Program, and they agreed: I looked like I belonged. The other parents pitched in and paid my entrance and participation fee to the ODP regional tryouts in Encino—just as they'd been paying my NSCAA and Select team traveling fees—and I rode out with Gwen and Alexis to the minicamp. After a long day, as we slipped out of our gear, Alexis told me that I'd been the best player out there that day. She'd been a little bit tentative, still rehabbing that knee, but when she went wide for a pass, I'd been looking for her, sending her good balls at pace.

"I love playing with you, True," she said, giving me that familiar smile as we headed in for our showers.

—

I was sitting against the outside wall of the PE offices, facing the swimming pool, eating chicken breast, and drinking unsweetened iced tea, when Coach Drixler walked over with his aviator sunglasses pushed up on his bushy red hair. He told me I'd been named first alternate for the ODP; Gwen and Alexis were officially in.

"What does that mean?" I asked.

"It means if someone gets hurt or can't make it to the program for whatever reason, you're going."

"But I played better at ODP tryouts than Gwen and Alexis."

Coach Drixler pursed his oily lips—he was always applying lip balm during practice—and said, "You can't say better, but you're definitely on their level."

"But they're not first alternates or whatever."

"Look, True, you're a super player, but you have a reputation."

"I'm a good teammate."

"To be a good teammate, you need to stay on the pitch. You get thrown off too much. You fight too much."

I put away the rest of my chicken breast and swigged my iced tea. "One fight," I said.

"One *this year*, and you broke that girl's jaw. And last year? And in regionals you've been carded how many times?"

"She was playing dirty," I said, ignoring his question about my red cards in regionals. "And she was going after Lorena's legs. I did that for—"

"Look, something will happen, someone will get hurt, and you'll get called up. Just don't blow it by being difficult. I like you, True. You're a useful player, very useful, but you need to tone down the aggression a little."

Two weeks later, it was determined that a girl from Oregon had been playing on a forged birth certificate and was actually two years older than her parents had claimed. Her spot went to me.

Chapter 6

Pauline's favorite food was white bread. She could eat a half dozen unbuttered slices, balling the bread up in her fists and biting into the clumps as if she were eating an apple. I encouraged her to vary her diet, but besides white bread, the only thing she took a liking to was white rice. So we developed a routine. I'd withhold the bread or the rice until she'd eaten some protein—a strip of chicken or steak—and some broccoli, and drank her juice. When I finally set out a bowl of rice, Pauline would try to eat it with her fingers before my father would take back the bowl, and Pauline's face would contort in anger; her lovely features—her pert little nose, her wide almond-shaped eyes—would narrow and purse, and her face would redden, and she would start rocking and shaking her head at the injustice of her carbs being withheld despite her having dutifully consumed her protein and chlorophyll.

"B-b-b-b-b-b-b-b," she would mumble, attempting to get out "bad girl," which she'd been called enough times to now use the phrase as her universal expression of protest.

My father would hold the bowl back and say, "Use your spoon."

"B-b-b-b-b-b-b—"

"Spoon. Pauline, use your spoon."

She would rock and shake, unable to understand the directions, until my father would point to the spoon, then to the bowl, then back to the spoon.

I could watch the thought process actually transpire, Pauline looking at the spoon, recognizing it, and then finally picking it up in her clumsy fingers. She was lacking in fine motor skills, so she clutched the spoon in her closed fist and then looked up expectantly for her bowl of rice.

There were stretches when it still felt like we would make it as a family. In the evenings, while other fathers walked their dogs, our dad walked Pauline. We didn't call it a leash, but that's what it was, a child's safety harness fitted around her abdomen. Pauline trailed after my father, twiddling her fingers, wearing a fake-leather jacket he had gotten her, and she would walk in her strangely stiff-legged walk, nodding her head, repeating her metronomic mumbling, still so beautiful that other grown-ups would smile when they saw her, until they got closer and clocked just how very odd this little girl was. I joined them some evenings, when my father would take a route along the cliffs near our house, the dirt path worn through the creosote bush. Our evening constitutionals, my father called them.

My legs were often sore from running, from practice, so I took careful steps in a pair of running shoes, looking down at the path, avoiding stones. My feet took enough punishment every afternoon on the pitch, getting stomped on, twisted, caught, and crushed, so I had become obsessed with avoiding unnecessary contact.

We made our way slowly. My father believed that the only way to ensure that Pauline would sleep more than a few hours was to make sure she was physically exhausted. No one at her school or day care made her run or do much exercise, so she usually just sat on the lawn or in the sandbox, twiddling her fingers during what were called "exercise" classes. Which is why my father came up with these evening walks, long loops through Pacific Point.

My father walked in his blue jacket with a plaid lining, hands in his pockets, his head angled slightly forward as if he was deep in thought. I walked behind him, eyes on the stones, and Pauline brought up the rear on the ten-yard lead my father held. The only time she broke into a trot and caught up with my father, clutching him desperately, was when a dog approached. She was terrified of dogs and would shake her head anxiously and try to cross the street at the sight of an oncoming canine.

"B-b-b-b-b-b-b-b."

"It's okay, Paul. It's okay."

My father took her arm and positioned himself between Pauline and the leashed hound.

As soon as the dog was out of sight, she let go, instantly unafraid.

Other than the occasional canine threat, she was happy on those walks, flashing a jack-o'-lantern of a smile, her straight teeth glistening in the last light. Her day, I realized, was filled with tasks and drills and conditioning, and like a dog confined to perpetual obedience school—or a youth soccer player during two-a-days—she enjoyed these few moments of freedom with her family, taking the same comfort in safety, in the pack, as any other mammal.

One evening, my father asked me about *Zen and the Art of Motorcycle Maintenance*, an old paperback he'd given to me that I hadn't read. I knew he was disappointed that I'd stopped reading, and I wanted to tell him, *Give me books about soccer, about* girls *playing soccer.* But besides some YA books about girls scoring the winning goal in the big match, there just weren't any.

"Sometimes I hate Pauline," I ventured one evening while we were walking. It was as if I just wanted to hear what those words sounded like, to know whether it was possible to say them out loud.

My father stopped and shook his head. He looked at me, understanding giving way to disappointment. "She's your sister."

"But sometimes, it's just . . ." I tried to make that point about siblings, about how other kids get to hate their siblings sometimes, about how other kids even get to hit their sisters or brothers sometimes, but I couldn't get it out.

"I'm so glad your mother isn't here to listen to that."

I shook my head and turned and walked back home, leaving the two of them to finish the route without me.

He saw it from his vantage point, I suppose, as a father who could never admit to himself that the burden of caring for my sister might take us all down. And already, so much of that burden was shifting to me. But I was getting a break, two spring weeks away at the Olympic Development Program, the ODP, to play with the best girls under seventeen in the United States. It didn't matter that I made it as an alternate (or it did, but it didn't): I was now one of the best thirty girls—or sixty, actually, as it turned out there were two national ODP camps—in the country. From this group, twenty-one girls would be invited to come back for the summer residency, where the national team pool was actually decided.

Chapter 7

Alexis, Gwen, and I met at the airport, clutching our duffels and backpacks, our parents dropping us off. My two teammates each had three inches on me, though I may have outweighed both, because where they were softening and rounding, I was becoming harder. No other NSCAA region in the country was sending three players to Colorado Springs for the camp. Gwen's mother would be coming along with us, though we would be staying in Air Force Academy dormitories, and Gwen's mom would be staying in a nearby hotel. Alexis's parents would follow a few days later because of her father's work commitments. The Olympic Development Program information packet that I'd received specifically said that parents did not need to attend. It never occurred to my father or to me that he would join me. They would send an assistant coach to the airport to pick up each girl, and there were female resident advisers on each hall where we were staying. Alexis and Gwen had already arranged to share a room, and I was assigned a girl from Washington named Jamilla as my roommate. Some of the girls who would later become famous for their national team play were attending the camp; some names you would recognize, but most of the girls were as anxious and nervous as we were.

We boarded the plane, and we all had a different way of hiding our anxiety. Gwen was giggling as she flipped through a copy of *Cosmo* and circled products she wanted. Alexis was thoughtful, discussing which girls we'd played against in regionals might pose a threat to us. I was in the middle seat and couldn't think of much to say. I was antsy but also thrilled, like the tension that had been building inside would finally get a chance to break. I was going to measure myself against the best. That's what I'd been waiting for. I didn't say this to Alexis, but I suspected she felt the same way. When, halfway through the flight, I realized I'd forgotten my chicken breasts at home, she shared her take-out sushi and peanut-butter granola bars with me.

Gwen's mother rented a car and drove us over to the campus. I checked in and found Jamilla in the dormitory common area, a little grouping of a dozen upholstered chairs with wooden arms and a pair of indestructible-looking coffee tables. She turned out to be a wiry girl with bleached white hair and a narrow, plain-featured face. I had heard of Jamilla; by then, most of us from the western United States had played against or with each other at different points in our careers, or had at least heard of each other. And because there were three of us from the same high school, everyone knew about Gwen, Alexis, and me. As Jamilla walked me down the hall to our room, she said she'd already staked out her bed but that there wasn't much difference between them. She'd been in Colorado Springs for four days, so she'd arrived at the facility as soon as the camp opened. I unzipped my duffel and removed my shoes and sweats, and then Jamilla said, "Wait. You're not going to believe this."

She opened the closet door, and it was filled with Olympic swag: tracksuits, sneakers, balls, shin guards, duffel bags, even gift certificates to Subway, the Nike store, and AMC theaters, and a Sony Discman.

I removed a pair of Nike cleats. They were my size.

"We have to wear these?" I asked. I preferred my Diadoras.

She shrugged. "If you make the team, I think probably. They have a deal."

That night all the girls piled into these open passenger wagons pulled by what looked like a tractor. They drove us down a sloping paved path and then across an empty two-lane road and up to a training facility called the Falcon Center. Inside was a team of doctors, physical therapists, and trainers, led by Dr. Gifford, a tall, short-haired brunette in a white lab coat who wore a pair of thick-framed glasses. She held a clipboard and welcomed us to camp, telling us she was the chief medical officer of the US Olympic Women's Soccer Team and that we would each have a quick induction physical before meeting the coach.

I took my turn in the cone of light in the middle of the training office, and Dr. Gifford stood near the door, studying me through her glasses. A pair of women in shorts and T-shirts ran a measuring tape along my thighs and around my legs and hips. They slid my stockinged feet into Brannocks, then my bare feet. Height. Weight. BMI. They took down everything, recording every inch of me, even the shape and size of my forehead, the distance between my thumb and pinky, the diagonal width of my palm, the ratio of my middle toe to my big toe. Blood type. Resting heart rate. Blood-oxygenation level. They drew a half dozen test tubes of blood, stanching the puncture wound with a cotton ball and adhesive cloth tape. I had several bruises, dark grape-juice stains on my calves, thighs, and stomach, and a contusion on my shin that was stubbornly slow to heal. They drew circles around each with a Sharpie and took Polaroids, and then wrote on the backs of the photographs the location of each wound. My battered feet were even more carefully considered, photographed, and documented. After that, Dr. Gifford listened to my heart, then listened to me breathing. She asked me to remove my panties and hop up on the training table, and then she slipped on rubber gloves. While she was casually inspecting my labia and then taking a pap smear, she asked when I'd first had my menses. Then she asked whether I was sexually active.

"No."

The assistants were busily scribbling on their clipboards.

She asked about my sister and my father, and nodded at my responses. Family history of heart disease, hypertension, mental illness?

Dr. Gifford said there was a note in my file recommending an MMPI test but that it was up to my father to sign off on that.

"What is it?" I asked.

"It's a test that assesses personality traits."

"Does every girl take one?"

Dr. Gifford took a breath and removed her glasses, then shook her head.

The next morning we met Coach Tony, a small man with a mop-top haircut that was just beginning to go gray. He spoke with a British accent and told us he was from Newcastle, England (we already knew this) and that he'd played a half dozen years in the First Division with Aston Villa (we already knew this, too). He said he had a simple philosophy: he was ball oriented, which meant that we, as a team, would keep possession, and when we didn't have the ball, we would get it back. The current fashion of counterattacking football didn't suit him or play to what he'd identified as our advantage as American women: our fitness. To keep the ball, he explained, we needed good players, twenty-one of them to be exact, but the problem, as he saw it, was that good players tended to be inefficient; they wanted to do pretty things with the ball instead of simple things.

"Simple beats pretty," said Coach Tony.

He told us he would elaborate more over the next thirteen days but that we should think of the entire pitch as a series of spaces and that when one of our teammates advanced out of a space ahead of us, we should look to move into that space, with or without the ball.

Empty space. That was something I understood.

He said this was one of two ODP camps. "Sixty girls to make twenty-one. But remember, this is a development camp. Even for those girls who aren't invited to residency camp or to the team, what you learn here will benefit you no matter what level of football you finally reach.

"You're all good players here. And I'm going to make you better. That's the only sure fact of the next two weeks."

Then a nutritionist talked to us about diet and fluid intake, about the importance of protein and high-fiber carbs in the morning. Black coffee was fine; tea was better; water best.

Breakfast was my first chance to size up the other twenty-seven girls. These were the best girls in the country, I thought, and then my next thought was this: I hated them. Each and every one. There, at the tables, were twenty-seven more Alexises, pretty girls with two-parent homes and normal siblings and boyfriends and BMWs. I pushed that out of my mind. Finally, here was a truly equal playing field. Money didn't matter here. Private coaching no longer mattered. Nothing mattered but what we did on the pitch.

Back in the common space, there was a fridge stocked with water and some sports drinks and snacks from companies that were sponsoring the United States Olympic Committee (USOC). Balance Bar had cut some sort of deal, and their candy bars were everywhere. Some of the girls lived on them, but after taking one bite of the cookie-dough flavor, I could tell they were garbage. I preferred the real food at the training table, and even though some of the other girls were already complaining after only one meal, I appreciated the variety of proteins. Chicken, steak, salmon, scrambled eggs—and this stuff was available until ten at night.

In the locker room we were assigned open lockers with our names in black stenciled letters on white plastic rectangles, and each was stocked with kit: jerseys, shorts, sports bras, leggings, headbands, pads, boots, all in our sizes. Most of us had brought our own boots, sensitive as we were about our feet, but the rest of it was a thrill, and as we stripped down, we revealed our bruised and contused bodies to each other for the first time. Naked, we were far more similar than different, especially with boobs taped down and pubes trimmed so that nothing showed out of our sports briefs. But as we dressed, there was a steady anxiety in the room, audible over the clicking of cleats and ripping of Velcro, the zip of laces being tightened.

My toenails were short and cut blunt; I clipped them nightly. I spent twenty minutes before practice taping my toes, then wrapping a sheath around my foot, then a short sock, then my ankle and shin guards, then two pairs of socks, and then sliding the whole package into my boots, and bending and prodding the foot to check if it felt right. Too thick, too bulky—I wouldn't feel the ball through my cleats. I slipped off the shoe and started the whole process all over again.

There was a light dusting of talcum powder in the air, the chalky motes swirling in the cold light reflecting off the concrete walls. I felt at home. The world outside of soccer started falling away. My sister, my mother, everyone else receded. I released the whole of my life's stresses, and I saw the next few hours, the next few weeks, narrowing to a pleasing focus. I'd first had this sensation when I played biddy ball, and though I hadn't been able to put it into words back then, I'd experienced that release. Ever since, I'd waited for it, and when it came—lacing my shoes, feeling around my toes to make sure they were comfortable, standing and bouncing up and down—I felt that whoosh of the bad exiting, and soon, I knew, I would feel nothing.

The practice pitch was where the Air Force Academy football teams usually drilled. They'd just completed their own spring practice, and the USOC had resodded the pitch for our camp. Perfect, dense Bahia grass trimmed to putting-green height so that the ball rolled but never skidded. As we came out onto the pitch, each of us pushed a toe into the ground instinctively, testing for firmness, for give. We bounced; we dug in a heel. Nice grass. Coach Tony was standing with a half dozen assistants, four women and two men, and they were each looking at a clipboard. As we gathered around, Coach Tony looked up at us as if surprised to find thirty soccer players on a soccer pitch.

"Stretch 'em out," he said to an assistant trainer, turning back to his colleagues. As we were led through some routine stretches, we could hear the coaches murmuring. Here or there we could make out a girl's name, but we had no way to understand if that mention was a good sign or a bad sign.

Coach Tony finally turned back to us. He was wearing a black jacket, black shorts, and a pair of black boots with high-top socks.

"You run six to seven miles playing a match," he said. "Now you're gonna run five."

He pointed to a track demarcated by stubby cones. Each lap was four hundred meters; five miles was twenty laps.

We looked at each other as if waiting for an order to go. "Tempo, girls. You've got thirty-three minutes."

En masse, we gathered and ran. Back home, I was used to being the first in suicides and hummingbirds, but here, I quickly fell into pace behind a half dozen girls who pushed out in front.

It was a bright day, dull yellow sun, roads ribboning up into distant mountains with silver-and-white jagged peaks. A pair of hawks circled overhead. Quickly, most of us were experiencing an unexpected shortness of breath, and it dawned on me: altitude. We'd been here less than twenty-four hours, and our lungs hadn't adjusted. After only two miles at a pace of six minutes per mile, I was gassed. Alexis and Gwen were even farther behind. Up ahead were at least a dozen girls, including Jamilla, who, I realized, was already acclimated, having arrived a few days ago. I closed my mouth, attempted to regulate my breathing, and accelerated into that top group. No way was I going to finish out of the top third, even if my lungs weren't yet used to the thin air.

I was familiar with pushing my body past the pain barrier, blowing through the depleted state where most of my teammates would give in and stop. Every hummingbird was a test of will, and one that I always passed. But today, in the thin air, this felt different, and each lap seemed like it might break me. After three miles, a few girls had noticeably slowed down, gasping, and the girls in the first group, in which I was taking the rear, had already lapped a pair of particularly hapless girls from Arizona who were obviously struggling. (Later, when Coach Tony asked one of them why she couldn't complete the run, she answered, "Asthma," and Coach Tony nodded sympathetically, said, "Oh, well then you should practice on the asthma field, right over there," and pointed toward the training center. We never saw her again.)

I puked after four miles, stopping for fifteen seconds, my hands on my knees. After barfing my breakfast onto the turf, I took off again.

I managed to finish eleventh, inside of thirty minutes, and I was too exhausted and sick from the run to feel any disappointment at my performance. I collapsed onto the grass with the others who'd already finished. Alexis trotted in a few seconds behind me and fell down next to me on the field; Gwen followed a couple minutes later. Only the girls who'd arrived at the camp days early were breathing normally.

After fifteen minutes' rest and rehydration, Coach Tony broke us into fives for small-goal scrimmages, three half-hour five-a-sides so that the coaches could make first-day assessments of our skills. I was assigned to one game, and Alexis and Gwen were grouped in another. It was Coach Tony's intention to exhaust us before seeing us play; many coaches believe you can see a player's true form when she is physically spent, when instinct and will replace technique and finesse, when she gives up goals because she is too tired to back and face, when she makes an easy pass rather than the right one, when a defender might commit a stupid foul instead of winning position on a player.

As soon as the ball was in play, I could tell that the other nine girls on the pitch were equal to the very best girls I'd played against in Select or NSCAA regionals, certainly better than the girls from any of the high school teams we'd played. They all possessed the basic technical tools and tactical awareness, and they played as well when their team lacked the ball as when they had the ball. Each had size, strength, speed, and stamina—in fact, I realized, looking around, I was the shortest player in this game.

We were all used to dominating the field, and even though our coaches, technical advisers, and every soccer camp we'd ever attended urged us to play hard from the beginning, we naturally took a few minutes to get a sense of what kind of effort, exactly, was required here. The girls were all quick, and each had that knack that a good footballer has of playing easy yet fast—that is, few touches, good runs, great distances covered in an instant. If I lost my girl on defense for a blink, she was gone and receiving an easy pass in front of the goal. Within five minutes of the ball rolling in, we knew what we were up against.

The game quickly ratcheted up to a higher intensity than almost any game I'd ever played in before. Any pretense of friendship was dropped, and the girls started barking at teammates or pushing off opposing players. One girl on our team, a tall brunette from Texas, was repeatedly dribbling into the teeth of this defense, her head down, unwilling to look for her teammates, and I was about to tell her to fucking pass the ball when another of my teammates hissed at her, "Give up the ball, bitch." After that we settled down into something resembling positional soccer, each of us operating in a specific zone on the field and taking turns attacking and then coming back when gassed to play last girl in front of our goal. Soon, I was no longer even aware of the coaches watching us, or of Coach Tony coming over and standing behind our goal. I was thinking only of the four girls I was playing with, any of whom I would have gladly gone into battle with.

I felt I was acquitting myself well, particularly in the back half, where my decision-making—when to go forward, when to fall back, when to make a hard challenge, when to risk a foul—all felt natural and comfortable, though more than a few times I heard the other girls complaining about my hard play.

"*¡Puta!*" shouted a Latina girl from Nevada as I forced her off the ball.

"*¡No fue falta!*" I said. *I will fight any bitch for the ball. And I will win every ball. 'Cause every bitch is in my world now.*

After a half hour, the coaches brought us in, saying nothing about what they'd seen and showing no indication as to whether they were pleased with our play. I found Alexis and Gwen, their faces red and sweaty, bits of grass on their arms and foreheads. Gwen was already bleeding from her elbows. I smiled. Gwen looked a little shaken by what she'd seen, just this half hour of scrimmage, as if the competition was a little tougher than she'd imagined. I was just grateful I'd finally found girls as mean as I was—on the pitch.

Next, Coach Tony broke us up into two groups and had us run set- and through-ball drills, passing set drills and turning drills, all of it done at pace. Now the coaches were critiquing us, looking out for extra steps, for a clumsy turn, for a wayward ball, for a slow ball.

"This isn't a fucking tap dance," Coach Tony shouted at Jamilla. "You should have turned and reset before the ball came back to you. You look like a bloody showgirl with all those dance steps."

Coach Tony hated unnecessary movement, despised the extra touch, the extra step; he loved a one-touch set and through ball, hips swiveling to level, a through pass between the cones at full speed. And if the girl receiving took a bad line, instead of blaming the passer, he knew it was the cutter's fault. "Where the hell are you running to?" he shouted. "Two points. Shortest distance. Straight line. It's bloody simple, but the simple thing is always the hardest."

—

I slept like a baby at night, exhausted, my legs sore, even after the post-workout rubdown. We drank so much water that we were each up every hour to pee, yet we still woke up feeling dehydrated. We ate bananas and dates every morning to stockpile potassium, but it didn't matter; we finished every practice cramping from dehydration and two pounds lighter than when we had come out in the morning.

We were always watched. Even when we were in the dining hall with its Falcons logo on the ceiling, we could see the coaches observing us, seated at their table or standing, convening quietly, looking up periodically, and then nodding and talking some more. We were already conditioned to self-critique, but it became impossible not to obsess—about our own performances, about where we ranked, about where we stood in the coaches' estimation, in Coach Tony's judgment, even in Dr. Gifford's evaluations. Some of the girls were obviously nursing hamstring or calf strains, or hyperextended knees, but they avoided reporting to Dr. Gifford, worried that admitting an injury would get them sent home.

After a particularly grueling day of endless one-v.-ones, Y passing and finishing drills, tika-takas, the Barcelona Star passing pattern, eight-hundreds—brutal runs where you go full speed for a half mile, stop for twenty seconds, do another half mile, then rest, then do another, and so on—and a forty-five-minute five-a-side scrimmage (during which my left foot was badly stomped on by a freckled, red-haired girl named Michelle from Santa Clara), I took off my shoes in the locker room and saw that blood was building up under my left big toe. The pressure was starting to hurt. By the time we came back from dinner, my toe was throbbing, and I wasn't sure I'd be able to walk, much less play, the following day. Wary of approaching Dr. Gifford, I limped back to the kitchen, asked one of the cooks for a sharp carving knife—I said I needed to dice a mango—and then locked myself in my suite's bathroom. I punched a hole through the keratin on my left big toe and released the blood, which poured out of the crack and immediately lessened the pain. I sat there, breathing deeply, letting the blood run down my toe and surround my foot. Then I slipped on a sock and my slides, and walked back to my room as if nothing were wrong. The next morning, my sheet was all red, but my toe felt okay. I wrapped it in a bandage, slid on a sports sock, and determined that I could keep playing.

Coach made us run ten eight-hundreds that morning. When I came in after morning practice, my entire sock was red. But I never missed a minute on the pitch.

By the end of the first week, eight girls had been sent home.

Chapter 8

My father had signed off on the psych evaluation. The beginning of week two, Dr. Gifford pulled me aside after breakfast and told me to hang back so that I could take the Minnesota Multiphasic Personality Inventory. I asked her again why I was the only girl being singled out, and she said I wasn't. Other girls were taking it. When I asked who, she said she couldn't tell me. But the test was a valuable tool, she said, in determining team-first personalities, in trying to assemble the group of females who could live, travel, and play together.

She wasn't admitting it, but I knew I was being targeted because of my "issues." I'd gotten into too many fights, thrown too many elbows, been red-carded too many times—the same reason I'd had to sneak into the ODP through alternate status. Or was it because of my sister? Were they worried that some strain of crazy ran in the family and had infected me?

"There are no right answers," Dr. Gifford told me. "Just respond honestly." But I could tell that the 570 true-false questions did have right answers.

"I often feel hot with no apparent cause."

"I like to pick locks and take apart doorknobs."

"I see things or animals or people around me that others do not see."

"It would be better if most laws were thrown away."

This was a test to weed out the loonies. So as I sat and read, I made sure to circle the least offensive answer, to project a version of myself that was less violent on the pitch and more sociable in real life than I actually was.

The exam was scored while I was out at afternoon scrimmages. A sports psychologist working with the national team, Dr. Dorfman, had apparently checked in with all my coaches. And while my regional coaches had spoken highly of me, I could sort of tell that Coach Drixler had let the ODP people know that I was socially isolated. When Dr. Dorfman asked me to come and see her after dinner, I wanted to blurt out that my Pacific Point Sea Lionesses teammates had changed. We'd been friends all through middle school and Tri-County and Select, but somehow during high school I was no longer good enough for them. But I was wary of how this would sound.

Dr. Dorfman had black hair that fell to her shoulders, and she wore black jeans and a long-sleeved black sweater. Despite her being a psychologist, her skin looked sun-kissed, and she wore hiking boots even when she was in the training facility.

We met in a treatment room. There was a massage bench next to the metal-framed plastic chair in which I sat, and Dr. Dorfman faced me in a padded chair. She nodded at me and smiled, looking down at what I assumed were my test results.

"How is camp?" she asked. I told her I fucking loved it. "Making friends?"

I shrugged. No, I wasn't. But she probably already knew that.

"Are you anxious, uncomfortable?"

I shook my head. "I'm never anxious when I'm playing soccer."

"What are your goals for this next week?"

"Better first touch. To be the best in the daily fitness. Get invited to residency camp this summer."

She shook her head. "Can we add one more?"

"Sure."

"To avoid any disagreements or arguments on the pitch. A totally conflict-free week. How does that sound?"

I thought I'd just had a totally conflict-free week. "What do you mean? I haven't been fighting. I've been getting along and stuff."

"The coaches, Coach Tony, he's seen a few incidents."

I was confused. I thought I'd toned it down, kept to myself, avoided conflict.

"Some unnecessary rough play, hard fouls."

"I'm trying to make the team."

"These are your teammates—"

"I haven't punched anyone," I said.

Dr. Dorfman began scribbling in her folder.

"Wait, wait. Stop, stop writing," I said.

She kept scribbling.

"Stop," I shouted.

She looked up at me, cocked her head to one side, and began writing even faster.

"Listen to me," I said. "I won't—I'll be good."

But she'd already formed her opinion. I was a problem, a head case, and somehow, despite what I believed had been exemplary behavior, I had made a bad impression.

Alexis and Gwen had somehow formed a clique with a half dozen other girls, pretty girls like them, good players, sure, but girls who played in makeup and lipstick, who spent forty minutes before every game doing their hair. They would make up the photogenic core of the national team that would land on the cover of *Time* a few years later. While the three of us had arrived at the ODP together and managed to maintain cordiality for the first few days of camp, our relationship was badly fraying by the end of that first week. It was clear from how

Coach Tony was dividing up the scrimmages that he saw Alexis and me both playing the same position, offensive midfield, and we knew the USWNT (United States Women's National Team) that had won gold at the Atlanta Olympics already had Julie, Brandi, Michelle, Kristine, and Tisha, so midfield spots would be scarce in residence. Alexis and I were rivals now. I guess we always had been, but now we had to admit it.

Alexis had been wise, taking her time recovering from last fall's knee injury, playing sparingly in regionals and high school games. She still wasn't in full form, but she was nearly there. She'd been saving herself for this camp, which meant I was more game fit, but she had fresher legs. We'd been playing with each other for a decade, and we knew each other's tendencies so well that when Coach Tony lined us up opposite each other, the one-v.-one battles were epic. Alexis was a long player, and her interminable, slender legs and narrow feet efficiently flicked and tapped the ball like a spider wrapping a fly. She used her size to keep me off the ball. In the past, she could frustrate me, baiting me into coming around her for a ball that was no longer there. Now I was more patient and knew I could wear her down with physical play, a shove here and there, a forearm against her back, a lunge that brought our hips into hard contact. But if I got lazy, gave her any space at all, she could beat me with a good pass or even a turn and go to her left. Give her space down the left side and she could pick you apart, so I always pushed her to her right, into the heavier traffic in the middle, where she couldn't hide the ball at the end of her long legs. Still, despite my grinding her down, she beat me plenty of times that first week.

But she couldn't really stop me either. I was all sharp points—fists, wrists, elbows, knees, hips, forehead—and when she tried to close in on me, she got stung. Nothing too obvious, nothing the coaches could see, but after twenty minutes of a scrimmage, she was giving me a crucial foot or two of space, enough for me to see the field and find teammates for easy passes or to meg her.

Plenty of times, I left her behind me. “Bitch!” she would gasp as I found my way to the front of the goal.

The battles took on an intensity I’d never experienced before. Coach Tony spurred us on, complimenting one or the other, depending on the day or the situation. When one of us got the spotlight, the other got the shaft. I wondered if the coaches were intentionally trying to push me to the breaking point, to get me to lose my cool, to throw a punch, but outside of some rough stuff on the pitch, I believed I’d been a good citizen.

Midway through week two, Alexis and I were no longer speaking. Even in the dining hall, where we were all encouraged to sit together, there were dominant cliques and in-crowds. We were all high school girls, after all. I ended up at the end of the long table—far from Alexis, Gwen, and the glamour girls—seated with a couple of Latinas from Riverside and San Diego, impressive physical specimens who lacked the coaching or training to go much further. The irony of American women’s soccer being an almost exclusively Caucasian sport wouldn’t be widely noticed until the next century. We were American white girls playing what in the rest of the world is a brown man’s game. It had to do with financial resources, white families having the money to send their promising daughters to soccer camps and to hire technical advisers. Most Latino families, even those with talented daughters, lacked the scratch for this extra training. (Or they spent it on their sons instead of their daughters.) High school coaches just weren’t good enough to make you good enough. I had benefited from my friends’ parents’ desire to ensure their daughters were on winning teams. My fees were paid not out of the kindness of strangers but the competitiveness of strangers.

I chewed on my chicken breast, my black beans, my carrots and sweet potatoes, and listened as Ava and Nachia spoke in Spanish. The gist of their conversation was the same as any other: speculation about who would come back to rezzies this summer and who would be gone.

They said they thought I would be invited back for sure. I was one of the best players. As good, they said, as some of the USWNT girls. But I ignored their flattery. Girls here were either overly encouraging or discouraging, seeking to inflate or deflate an ego, to make a rival complacent or anxious. My goal was simple: ignore all the noise, come back to rezzies, then play in college.

One morning, the two Mexicans were gone. We were down to nineteen now. I sat by myself at the far end of the table. Alexis no longer looked at me.

—

At night, I woke because of cramps in my calves or sharp aches in my feet. Our bodies were maps of the bruises and bashes we'd taken, swollen in places, tender and soft in others, and as we walked, our joints, ankles, knees, and necks made sounds like a pepper mill grinding. We were all being systematically worn down by the training, the practices, and the constant scrutiny, with Coach Tony and Dr. Gifford probing for any weakness, mental, physical, or emotional. If we couldn't handle the pressure here, where practices were closed and nobody else was watching, how would we handle the Pan American Games? The Three Nations? The Olympics? The Women's World Cup?

Coach Tony made it clear that the Under-17 National Team that would play against Sweden in Palo Alto in May would be drawn from the best twenty-one at the ODP. Make that roster, we all knew, and you were on your way to the residency program and the USWNT; make the roster, and every college scout in the country would know your name. If you wanted to be a soccer player for real, then this was the straightest path there was.

So at night, all of us lay there, ignoring the pain, dreaming of the game, of future glory, but also of the disconsolation of a future outside of the national team development system.

We'd all been working toward this for most of our lives. And to be here, so close, one of the forty-nine best, only to fall short, would be more heartbreaking than to not have been invited.

I lay awake thinking I had nothing else.

There were pay phones in the lounge at the end of the hall, and we were given MCI phone cards so we could call home. My father said he and Pauline were fine. They missed me. They were proud of me. He told me that the *Pacific Point Post* had done a story about the three of us, Alexis, Gwen, and I, going to the ODP. The whole town was proud of us. What he didn't tell me, what I would find out later, was that they ran photos only of Alexis and Gwen. They didn't publish one of me.

Pauline didn't understand telephones. Hold one to her ear, and she would run away, shaking her head. Dad said she went into my room sometimes, looking for me. I could imagine her in there, rocking back and forth in front of my bookcases full of trophies.

"Why did you let them give me that test?" I asked my dad.

"They said it was normal," he said. "Why, was something wrong?"

I told him no, that everything was fine. I couldn't explain that I spent every day at the ODP thinking that other people knew more about me than they were letting on, that this suspicion was preventing me from being a good teammate, or a good fake teammate, as we were supposed to be.

I limited myself to one phone call every four days. A crucial part of the selection process was team bonding. We needed to be seen celebrating and applauding our teammates, even when each girl could be the one who'd take my place on the Under-17 National Team—even though her success would mean my failure. Yet when we were watching videotapes in the film room, I was supposed to jump up and down and cheer when Alexis made a good play in a scrimmage, even when I was the girl she had beaten. What the fuck? It was unnatural. But they were looking for team spirit, and that meant a giddy celebration of our own failures. Everyone cheering her own potential demise.

But at night, in bed, we were nineteen girls carefully going over the day's events, and each of us was calculating on some internal spreadsheet her successes and failures, rating every girl from one to nineteen, figuring exactly where she stood.

They pushed us until we couldn't go any more. We had bodies like middleweight boxers after a losing bout. We were bags of blood and bones, so beaten up that on the very last morning, two girls quit rather than face another day of eight-hundreds, drills, and scrimmages. Alexis never faltered; neither did I. But by the end of it, instead of having a grudging mutual respect, instead of saying that after all this we could go back to being whatever we were before, we couldn't stand each other. I saw Alexis only as a force that was in my way—a beautiful monster between me and the goal.

The remaining girls met for one last time in the coaches' lounge, where Coach Tony and Dr. Gifford told us how proud they were that we seventeen girls had made it all the way through camp. The self-selection, they told us, was part of the process. Coach Tony said to look around this room and recognize our achievement, to take a moment to compliment each other, to praise our teammates. Which was more of that fake positive stuff, because there was another ODP camp coming up and another thirty girls would be arriving two days after we departed. Coach Tony would choose the twenty-one girls coming to rezzies from the best of both groups. Which meant that when we looked around the room, we knew that we couldn't all be invited to rezzies. For an unlucky few of us, this was it, the high point of our soccer careers.

Alexis, Gwen, and I flew back together, our flight and seat reservations made weeks ago. Gwen and Alexis took the window and middle. I took the aisle. Gwen and Alexis talked quietly to each other the whole flight. I didn't exchange a word with them the whole way.

Chapter 9

I flew up to Palo Alto in May to play on the Under-17 National Team against Sweden. Gwen and Alexis took a separate flight.

We were among the final twenty-one out of the original sixty, and I told myself I never doubted it.

But when we got there, instead of Coach Tony, we were met by one of his assistant coaches from the Olympic Development Program, Coach Katie, a freckled woman who wore her hair in a high ponytail and tended to clasp her hands as she spoke. We were staying at a Sheraton, and she called us all into her room, nearly two dozen of us crammed into every possible nook and cranny and corner, girls on top of girls, pushed up against each other. Some of us knew each other from ODP; others we'd never seen before—they must have come from the second ODP camp.

"Look around, girls," Coach Katie said. "In five days, you're representing your country against one of the best teams in the world. We have five days to make a team of you, and you have five days to convince me you belong on this team."

Who were the first eleven? How many of these girls were offensive midfielders? I looked around. The best players from our ODP camp were there, but I was surprised at one or two absences.

Girls vanished, disappeared: shredded ligaments, broken legs, broken spirits.

I racked with a girl named Daniela in a room with a view of a parking lot. We had breakfast coupons, and the next morning we went downstairs and sat quietly over eggs and turkey bacon. She was from Santa Clara, just a few miles from here, but we'd played against each other several times, even facing off in an NSCAA regional final that the Point Dynamo played against Santa Clara AC, a game we ended up winning 2–1. She'd been the best player on the other team, but as we sat there, eating our breakfast, I had trouble making small talk. Daniela chattered away about the upcoming five days, about playing Sweden, about rejoining the Under-17s, and I pushed my food into my mouth with my fork. This was her third game on a national team, she said, and she seemed positive that she'd be starting as a defender.

"Coach Katie loves me," she said confidently, buttering whole-wheat toast.

She asked me about Alexis. She'd emerged as one of the top girls in the ODP, and even the girls in the second ODP camp had heard about her. Alexis was talented and pretty. She was a model.

"They're looking for that, you know," said Daniela, who was already made up with eyeliner, lipstick, and tinted sunscreen. "To find girls who have a certain look, who not only can play but can, you know, help make the game more popular."

I didn't say it, but I thought it: *That's fucking ridiculous.*

At the first practice, held on the intramural fields on the Stanford campus, we were put through the same fitness routines we'd gone through in Colorado, only with more emphasis on full-field scrimmages and one-v.-ones. There was no superstar in this group, no Messi or Mia Hamm, no player who exuded that look-at-me quality. Instead, we were nineteen or so position players, very similarly matched in terms of skill, talent, fitness, speed, and strength. We were the best high school players in the country. And what would separate one of us from another would be how monstrous we could be. I would never lose a one-v.-one. I would always be at the top in fitness. Nobody on this team would ever outrun me or outwork me.

I imagined the camp was like a prison yard and I had to be queen bitch. My resolve and anger were a surprise even to me, and in those first couple of days, there were times that Coach Katie or one of the assistants would pull me aside and tell me to take a moment or two to settle myself, to calm down. One afternoon, Dr. Dorfman, the sports psychiatrist from the Olympic Development Program, appeared on the sidelines, wearing her hiking boots, brown with black soles, and a pair of mirrored sunglasses. She pulled me out of set- and through-ball drills and asked me to take a walk with her.

"How are you doing, Trudy?"

Fucking great, I wanted to tell her, *fucking fantastic. I will claw to death any girl who gets in my way.* "Fine," I said.

"Coach Katie says you're really making an impression."

I nodded.

"She also says you're playing a little rough, that there are issues with other girls."

What? No, not this. Not again.

"Are you making friends?" she asked. "Do you remember that piece during ODP where we talked about collegiality? Playing incident-free?"

I shook my head but said, "Yeah, sort of."

"You don't have to answer this," Dr. Dorfman said. "But do you have a therapist at home, someone you see, a counselor?"

I told her I didn't.

"Maybe look into that, finding someone you can talk to, about the issues in your life, your sister, your mom. A lot to unpack."

I felt like tackling her right there, like putting an elbow into her fucking gold hoop earring, like raking her ankle with my cleat. Instead, I said I would do that.

She said she had a list for me.

I didn't ask who was supposed to pay for that.

We scrimmaged against the Stanford women's varsity team twice, and I started in the second game. These were college girls, but the primary difference between the teams wasn't age but how well these girls knew each other and could play with each other. I quickly clocked their game style—build up from the back, then wide balls, then flood the box—but the rest of our girls seemed lost, and when we played, we looked like a bunch of children chasing after the damn ball. We had no shape whatsoever. I played well enough that game that Coach Katie left me in for the full scrimmage, which was about seventy minutes, before we called it. My one goal was a header on a long cross, a springy leap, shoulders clenched, mouth set, head swung violently to make hard contact with the ball, changing its trajectory so abruptly it froze the Stanford keeper. The goal was the cap on a tremendous performance, one that was overshadowed, it turned out, by a hard foul on Christy Stoffel, one of the Stanford team's most popular players and a cocaptain. She jumped up and immediately got in my face about it, and when I shoved her, she was so stunned at being pushed by a high school girl that it took a moment or two before she spat out that I played like a fucking truck driver.

"What does that even mean?" I asked.

"Everyone knows you're a fucking psycho. Stop playing like one."

I shook my head. "You're getting pushed around by a high school girl, is that it? You're out here fucking ball watching."

And then she shoved me. I fell back. The official sent us both off, and while I was sitting by myself at the edge of the bench, I saw Coach Katie and Dr. Gifford deep in conversation, and fuck, if I hadn't done it again. But what the hell did she mean? Everyone knows? Everyone knows what?

They gave Alexis the start against Sweden instead of me, and Coach Katie told me they almost didn't let me have the cap, were considering sending me home, but that on balance I had played so well, and against a collegiate team no less, that they were letting me stay as a substitute. My first match for my country, and I was unlikely to see any minutes, but at least I was there, the whole game, at the opposite end of the bench from Coach Katie, cheering and pretending to celebrate every fucking play of a 1–2 loss to Sweden, knowing that I could have helped my team, knowing that I was better than any player out there, knowing that I was so much better than Alexis. But I smiled the whole game. Or at least I thought I did.

Chapter 10

After the ODP and the Under-17 game against Sweden, we had to return to high school. High school soccer season was over, but Select and NSCAA games continued, and Point Dynamo was in the regionals again. It didn't matter as much to me or to Alexis as it once had, since we'd both played for the Under-17 National Team and had both set our sights so much higher, but soccer is soccer and I'm a slut for the game, so I never missed even a practice. I hightailed it from the field to Pauline's day care center, got her home, made dinner or picked up dinner from Hops, and washed my own sweaty kit and gear.

The letters started arriving from college programs, the best in the country: Wake Forest, UNC, UCLA, Florida, Virginia Tech, Portland, Stanford. They were inviting me for one of my five NCAA-allowed visits. I sorted through the letters and flipped through a US News & World Report college guide to read about the campuses, but all I really thought about were the soccer teams, who would play where, where the other Under-17s were planning to go. I wanted to win and to have fun, in that order. I didn't care about the brochures featuring the academic opportunities available to me at University X. I'd barely survived AP European History, AP US History, and AP Bio. I wasn't looking for academic challenges. My goals were to literally score goals.

The problem, of course, was money. We couldn't pay a nickel. Though I'd overcome my shame of discovering that my teammates' parents had been pooling their dollars to pay for my travel on our regional team, I was still hesitant to press these schools for exactly how generous they planned to be. Strangers or near strangers had been paying for my soccer for years, and I knew that the only way I could continue to play was through a college scholarship, the national team, or the other NSCAA families. Somebody always paid to get me out there because they needed me. Well, not me, but my game. The moment they stopped needing me, they wouldn't write those checks. It was like that for every young athlete.

I reread the letters closely. Nobody was offering me a full ride (yet), but it was clear from the tone of each of the coach's letters that I'd reached another level of desirability. If I reciprocated the interest of any particular college, that coach could discuss with me exactly how she'd make an education at her university possible. My high school guidance counselor and high school coach would then get into the specifics of the offers. They promised me, and I trusted them.

My father was also making plans for Pauline, talking about a facility in Gardena where she might, as he put it, "get the care she needs." He mumbled that we needed to find a home for her, and I was like, *We have a home, right here*, but I understood what he meant. My departure seemed inevitable, and even though I'd been gone for only a handful of weeks—first with the regional team, then the ODP, and then the national team—he'd been shorthanded around the house. He never begrudged me my absence, but when I returned I could tell how tired he was. No one knew better than I did how Pauline could wear you down.

My father occasionally asked me about friends, about boys, and wondered if there was anyone special. These were awkward conversations. We had never even discussed my period. I had ridden a bicycle down to the pharmacy, bought my own box of tampons, and spent fifteen minutes figuring out what to do with one—I did it all my damn self and never told anyone it had happened. The first time a gynecologist had seen me was at the ODP. When my dad asked about my social life, Pauline liked to listen in, pausing from her new favorite activity, drawing on sheets of white paper, simple, repetitive, symmetrical shapes, exercises she'd been taught to make her fingers stronger. She made sixty trapezoids on a page, starting on the outside borders and then drawing them in descending order of size until they were no larger than a bullet point. A page of trapezoids, all virtually symmetrical.

Pauline had been making slow, incremental progress—but progress, and not just in her hand-eye coordination. Or was it just our wishful thinking? No, she had. She knew more words, a couple hundred by now, but you had to really listen to her to hear them. She'd become fascinated by my makeup—not a very impressive collection, more a dabbler's palette for experimentation—and was proficient at brushing mascara onto her eyelashes, though she also once took a bite out of my lipstick. Neither of us, it seemed, knew what to do with makeup. I, of course, had to teach myself to apply lipstick, to draw on eyeliner, to wash my hair, to use conditioner. My father, as if trying to make up for his inability to pass on these tribal rituals, occasionally brought home a copy of *Mademoiselle* or *Cosmo*, as if these teen bibles could somehow make up for the lost wisdom never imparted by my dead mom. He once, early on in my puberty, gave me a book about how women masturbate entitled *It's Not Wrong to Love Yourself.* That was the extent of our conversation about human sexuality.

Pauline's great breakthrough to normalcy, of course, was unlikely, a distant shore never nearer. We knew, or we had to know, right? Or could we keep lying to ourselves? But when the three of us huddled around our kitchen table, hot afternoon wind dying down outside, the shadow of the eucalyptus tree extending its dark hand over our little cottage, it was easy to pretend we were a normal family, and I fell into the fantasy and told my father and Pauline that yes, there was a boy, maybe a boyfriend, who knew? But someone special. Yes, I was part of it, life, the dappling stream, that current, necking in cars, hickeys. I wasn't just some freak who played soccer; I was a complete girl.

At school Alexis and I ignored each other. She passed me in the hallways as if I were foul air. During Dynamo practices, our relationship degenerated into open hostility.

Her knee was completely healed and she was as fast and efficient as ever, and I no longer had any physical advantage over her. We remained perfect foils on the pitch and off it. She was beautiful, while I was plain. Alexis had always been the complete package: looks, brains, style, fitness. All I had was soccer.

She'd broken up with Brendan, or so I heard. The two of them must have been too good-looking to stand each other. Lorena, the closest thing I had to a friend from our core group of seven, passed along some other rumors, too: that Alexis was considering Stanford and University of North Carolina; that Gwen had visited Santa Clara; that other teammates, even those who hadn't made the ODP, were already narrowing their options—Pomona, Wake Forest, Texas. These girls had the means for as many visits as they liked. Only visits paid for by the schools themselves counted as one of the five official visits.

Lorena said she was considering UC Miramar, a Division II school. "I'll get more playing time."

But where would I go? She told me that since we came back from Under-17s, everyone was talking about how Alexis and I had been the two best players there. I could go wherever I wanted.

I shrugged and headed over to Coach Drixler's office. I told him I was more focused on residence. On making the Under-17s, playing the friendly against China, the Three Nations tournament. He said I had to focus on college. My priority should be getting an education. Soccer wasn't a career, he reminded me.

I knew that. We weren't men. There was no Major League Soccer for us. There were only those few slots abroad, professional leagues for women in Germany, Norway, Sweden, and Japan, but here in the United States, nothing. It was as if we didn't exist once we finished college. There was the national team, those girls already on posters on teenage girls' bedrooms: Brandi, Mia, Michelle, Tiffany, Joy, Kristine. But if you weren't on that roster, you were gone. Lucky if you could make a few kronor playing for some umlauted Swedish club in front of twelve hundred shivering fans.

That's why Drixler was so insistent that I consider my education first, soccer second—because, as the cliché went, your education is yours forever; soccer is only temporary. But bullshit, soccer was the only place I had ever felt any sense of permanence, of belonging, of being who I was supposed to be.

I told this to the therapist Dr. Dorfman recommended to me, an earnest lady in a medical-services building across the street from an IHOP, after she told me that her goal was to create a safe place where I could be myself. I wanted to tell her I already had a safe place, the soccer pitch, where I was totally fucking myself, but I held back.

She smelled like patchouli.

I asked her whether she was reporting any of this back to Dr. Gifford or Dr. Dorfman. The USWNT was paying for the sessions, after all.

She shook her head. This was confidential. Only if I posed an immediate threat to myself or to others would anyone be informed of any of our conversations.

Well, okay.

I didn't believe in therapy, but I described a picture that was more or less true: a girl, tightly wound, who had only one thing, soccer, but who seemed to fuck up enough that the one thing was occasionally taken away.

She asked what I did to precipitate this removal.

I told her I hit people. Or pushed them. Or kicked them. Or hurt them.

"You're violent?"

I shook my head. "I want to win."

"But these acts are perceived as violent."

I explained that in a game situation, or a practice, or a scrimmage, or even a drill, I would do anything to beat my opponent. That's what made me the best. She asked if I ever hurt myself.

I told her that I would never hurt myself, or that I would only if it were necessary.

"Necessary?"

That's when I mentioned how I'd eased the pressure on my big toe by punching a hole in the nail with a kitchen knife.

She didn't understand, and I had to explain it again. The pressure, the throbbing, the blood. I didn't have any choice.

She didn't say anything, but I got the feeling that I'd said something concerning, and I immediately regretted telling her about my toe.

She prescribed a medication called Serzone. I was to take one a day, every day.

Chapter 11

The boys' soccer team was throwing a house party, so everyone on the girls' team was invited. Lorena convinced me to go, helped me choose an outfit. I was nervous about seeing Alexis, until I realized I didn't need to worry, because Brendan was going to be there. Apparently, she didn't want to see him. Lorena and I pulled up to the house, a two-story Cape Cod, and walked through the half-open door.

I looked around, greeted a few of my teammates, a little self-conscious at the knee-length slit skirt Lorena had zipped me into—one of my mom's, it was that old—and the heels I had managed to cram my mangled feet into. (Oh, if only Dr. Gifford cared as much about the well-being of my feet as she did about my brain.) Master P and Tupac blasted through the stereo, but then suddenly the hip-hop switched off and on came old music by Guns N' Roses and newer stuff like "Semi-Charmed Life" by Third Eye Blind, and then the rock was switched off and the hip-hop came back on. The boys' team was celebrating a city semifinals run—a season that would have been considered a disappointment for the Sea Lionesses. There was only one player out of all of them with a chance to play Division I soccer, and he wasn't even there. He'd left as soon as the season ended for a skills camp in the Netherlands where he could train in the Ajax system.

I quickly walked through the living room and into what looked like another living room.

The kitchen glistened with stainless-steel appliances and stone countertops on which kids were playing quarters. I was handed a red plastic cup of cranberry juice and vodka, and then I wandered out front, where I sat on the retaining wall, my back to the house. Lorena came out trailing a boy named David, who occasionally followed her around and whom she'd dated at one point.

"You're so pretty in that skirt," Lorena said. She was slurring her words; her breath smelled of the vodka punch.

I nodded. Whatever. Fake praise. "Take a look at my nose, girlfriend."

"It's cute," she said. "It's got this, like, little bent part. Boys are saying you've become kind of hot."

Cute? This broken schnoz?

There was a Volkswagen GTI driving up and down the street, revving its engine, the driver burning rubber, braking to a halt a quarter mile or so up the road, and then turning around and doing the same thing coming back down, stereo blaring loud guitar rock I didn't recognize. The driver finally came to a halt and double-parked on the street a few feet from me. I could see it was Brendan, of Alexis and Brendan, drunk and red-eyed, grinning, nodding.

"You comin' in?" someone shouted from the doorway.

Brendan shrugged. He managed to communicate complete indifference and disdain for the gathering despite the fact that he was drag racing up and down the street in front of the very same party. He scanned the front yard, and his eyes settled on me. He pointed with his thumb and forefinger, like a pistol firing. Then he opened his car door and got out, leaving his engine idling in the middle of the street.

"You!" he said.

Lorena and David wandered away, as if they didn't want to see what would come next.

"Me," I whispered back.

Brendan had a canine mandible, long and jutting, a Joker smile, a pronounced nose with perfectly tapered nostrils, stern eyes, and a prominent upper brow that made him look far more thoughtful than he could possibly be. His head was long and sleek, a bullet rising to his freshly cut, spiked blond hair. He was, by the prevailing high school aesthetics of that time, beautiful—and stoned.

I didn't know whether Alexis had sent him here as some sort of emissary, or whether he even knew who I was.

"Alexis hates you," he said.

Okay. He knew. I nodded.

"You hate her?" he asked.

I shrugged.

"I do," he said.

He forced a quick laugh that came off more like the honking of a goose. "Let's get a drink," he said. "They have alcohol?"

"Vodka punch," I said, holding out my cup. "Here. I'm not gonna drink it."

He took it, drank it down, and said, "Okay, now let's get a drink."

He pulled me up by the arms and then sort of marched me ahead of him, up the walkway and the short flight of stairs and back into the house, where the hip-hop had now been replaced by an old Pearl Jam song. There seemed to be a war going on for control of the music.

Brendan walked through the house, high-fiving some of the soccer players, who seemed confused to see me by his side instead of, I guess, Alexis.

Rod, a varsity defender, handed Brendan a forty-ouncer of Schlitz, and Brendan took it, reaching behind for me and pulling me up the stairs with him.

"Where are we going?" I asked.

"Get you drunk," he said.

"I don't really drink," I told him. "And this is weird. And your car is just sitting there."

"Fuck, you're right." And he turned around and led me back downstairs and into his car, and the whole time I was thinking, *This is a bad idea,* but also thinking, *I've never wanted anything more in the world than to ride in this car with Brendan and go wherever he wants to take me.*

He took me to his house, up a canyon from the ocean, a one-story ranch style across the street from a cliff. His parents weren't home, or they were asleep—I couldn't figure out which—and we stood for a few minutes in his darkened kitchen, a gleaming refrigerator reflecting the incorrect green digital time from a microwave oven. Brendan poured vodka into glasses, mixed in orange juice, handed one to me, and studied me, blinking, as if trying to figure out exactly what I was doing there.

"I'm buzzed," he said.

But he wasn't that drunk—I could tell. He just said it as an excuse, as some sort of cover for what he was planning to do, which I didn't understand but knew I wanted to happen.

"You've become sort of, I don't know, cute," he said. "I mean, not that you weren't, but—"

"It's okay," I told him. "You don't have to bullshit me."

"No, I'm not," he said. "You're like, unique. You have this face like you're always angry, and your nose is, like, perfectly not perfect, and the freckles, like spotted, but it's sexy—"

And then he sort of swarmed me, a lunging, awkward gesture that mashed lips against lips, and he pressed me back against the counter, and I felt his hands all over me at once, arms, breasts, hips, ass, and then up my skirt, lifting the front. This was the first time anyone besides myself had touched me there (other than the doctor at the ODP camp), and at first it felt medical, as if he were checking that everything was all right, and for an instant I stopped breathing, as if this were an inspection I might not pass. But then he found what he was looking for.

Brendan was my first, right there in the kitchen. I desperately wanted to explore his body, but there was a greater urgency to this act somehow, and he lifted my skirt, lowered my panties, and removed them over my heels. He felt me, and thank god for soccer: I was always trimmed.

Then he stopped, fumbling for something, opening a plastic package.

"Come on." I pushed against him. "Do it. Come on."

I had fantasized about this for years. All the *Cosmo*s and *Mademoiselle*s, the tips and picks and dos and don'ts, the secrets to the hottest looks in the top videos on *TRL*, the "do me" eyes and "kiss me" lips—it had all been for Brendan. Sparkle. Blush. Foundation. Deodorant. "How Sporty Girls Can Also Look Sexy: 10 Post-Sweat Styles." In that moment of anticipation, I had two concurrent thoughts: *This is what I've been wanting* and *How in the world can this be happening?*

I was tempted to stop everything, lower my skirt, ask him why, but then I thought for a moment and realized why—of course, he'd seen me play. He'd seen me at my most beautiful.

Or he was drunk.

Or he wanted to get back at Alexis.

I didn't know how to have a relationship, how to be a girlfriend, nor did I necessarily want that, but I did want Brendan. And over the next few weeks, he became my first regular sexual partner, a gorgeous boy, more lovely than I had any right to have anticipated. This was the first stretch of unqualified happiness in my life off the pitch. I even began skipping Point Dynamo practices to spend afternoons with Brendan before I had to go and pick up Pauline.

My bedroom windows looked out onto a lemon tree, still heavy with fruit from the previous year, even though new white flowers were coming in. I tidied a little before he came over, which meant shoving my soccer gear into a closet, but he didn't care about my mess. He never led me to believe that this was anything permanent; rather, Brendan was passing between stations. Alexis was his last, and some other beautiful girl would be his next, and here I was, the static in between. Or that was all I allowed myself to believe. But in my single bed, the white flowers at my window, Brendan gave me an enthusiastic initiation. He seemed to like having the upper hand, and then, when our afternoons wound down, he'd dress quickly and leave. There was no small talk; there was just practical fucking—and more fucking—and then he was gone. And I would drive to day care to pick up Pauline.

Leaving the party together had caused some small commentary among our classmates, but when I started skipping practice, now, that really raised alarms. I'd never missed practice. My NSCAA coach, Mauricio, called the house after three missed practices to ask where I was. I told him I wasn't feeling well, intimating a female problem, and he hesitated to challenge me on that—always a problem for a male coach of female players—and told me to get back as soon as I could.

But when I returned to the state park where we practiced, the old polo field of some dead actor, I found that at least half of my teammates had turned on me. Alexis, apparently, had figured out what I'd been doing with my afternoons—gossip from the party, a drive by my house, Brendan's car parked out front, it was an easy case to make. Only Lorena continued to acknowledge me off the pitch.

Fine. I'd been ostracized before, and I would be again. I was the best midfielder on the team. Our best formation was me in the center midfield and Alexis to my left—otherwise, our midfield was like four girls standing in a semicircle, passing the ball around, no one to carry it or make a run or break down the defense. But suddenly, Alexis and I couldn't play together. We couldn't even look at each other.

Within ten minutes, Coach Mauricio pulled us aside and asked what was wrong. "Why aren't you getting on the front of each other's balls anymore?"

We both shook our heads. Nothing was wrong.

What had been a simple battle for a position on the national team had now turned into something deeper. And for the first time, Alexis saw me not only as a rival on the pitch but as a rival in life. Me? Imagine that.

Chapter 12

I was invited to rejoin the Under-17s for the friendly against China. The week before my scheduled departure, I drove Pauline to get Chinese food at a strip mall restaurant in Santa Monica. I could've just gone to Hops, but I wanted to make the occasion special, to make Pauline feel special. I put her in a pair of my old jeans that fit her perfectly and a strappy top, and then had her sit on a stool in the bathroom while I did her makeup. I expected her to bounce and rock and shake, but she was captivated by the brush against her face, and as I painted and applied my limited repertoire, Pauline smiled and made her best effort to restrain herself. She ran off only twice for a gallop around the living room, and each time she came back, bobbing her head. "M-m-m-m-m-more."

The makeup was superfluous—it didn't make an already very pretty girl any prettier—but she loved it. When she was dressed and then standing in front of the mirror, I took an entire disposable camera's worth of photos and promised we would drop the camera off at the pharmacy on the way to dinner.

She wanted sweet-and-sour pork and rice, and I would let her have as much apple juice and soda as she wanted. I even let her climb into the front seat, confident she wouldn't throw her shoes out the window or try to pull the emergency brake. She was that happy.

Brendan drove up as I was walking around to the driver's side. His flat stomach, barbed rib cage, and upper body were visible through the window of his GTI. "Damn, True, your sister is—"

"I don't want to hear it," I said.

He nodded. "So?"

"I'm busy," I told him. "Tomorrow?"

When I got in the car next to Pauline, she smiled, nodding and mumbling, "B-b-b-b-b-boyfriend."

I shrugged, and for the first time maybe ever, I felt like Pauline was annoying in the way every other little sister might be, and not just in the specific way that she excelled at.

I was taking her to a special dinner because in a few days, before my own departure, I'd be packing a suitcase full of Pauline's clothes and escorting her to a group home in Gardena. My father and I had gone around and around on this, arguing the point repeatedly. I maintained that we could still handle Pauline at home, that this wasn't fair to her. But he pointed out that I'd be leaving again in a few days for the Under-17 minicamp and the match against China, and then I would be gone for the summer because of residency, so who was supposed to take care of Pauline, especially during the summer, when her regular school ended and there was nothing but a few hours of day care a day?

Four days later, I was packing some of Mom's best dresses in with Pauline's scraps and odds and ends. I loaded a makeup pouch full of some of my best eyeliners, blushes, and lipsticks, my most precious items, hard won from scrounged dollars and twenties pilfered from Dad's wallet while he slept off a night at Hops. I was crying as I packed for her. Dad seemed grateful that I was helping and urged me to make sure everything on the checklist was also going into the suitcase: the more pedestrian medications, toothpaste, toothbrush, underwear, diapers (if necessary), favorite stuffed animals, et cetera. I busied myself with preparations while Pauline watched, rocking slightly, rapt at how carefully I loaded everything.

"C-c-c-c-camp," Pauline said.

She recalled that I'd gone away to the ODP, which she had called camp, and now she was going to her own camp, or so we'd framed it.

But her camp was, of course, permanent. She wasn't trying out for the developmentally disabled team. She'd already made it, no question. Dad just couldn't bring himself to tell her it was permanent. He said it was a trial, just a few weeks to see how she liked it. I'm not sure she understood the full implications of this project.

For my part, and I still felt guilty admitting it to myself, this seemed like an opportunity for me to finally become normal, to feel normal. Look how my life was progressing: I had a boy. I was heading to my second national team appearance and was likely to play this time, provided I didn't get into any altercations during minicamp. I felt so optimistic that I decided to stop taking the medication prescribed to me, though I didn't tell my therapist about that, fearing she might take that news as proof of some sort of return to the bad old me.

By the time we got to Gardena, I convinced myself that this was the best for all of us, that we all had to leave home eventually, either slightly damaged, like me, or more damaged, like Pauline. Everyone was pushed from the nest. Pauline was just a little less prepared for it than most of us. She was about to move in with a dozen other special-needs teenagers, eight boys and four girls, two to a room, supervised by a full-time staff of three during the day and two at night.

The president of the organization that ran the assisted-living facility, Found Horizons, greeted us as we arrived in the old Volvo, making sure to give Pauline a hug, which she, of course, didn't reciprocate. Pauline wasn't a hugger. We registered, found the room, unpacked Pauline's cheap clothes and her makeup, hung a few of Mom's old dresses in the closet, and folded as much as we could into her allotted pair of dresser drawers. She was sharing her room with a black-haired girl, Carmen, who wore a helmet and was even less verbal than Pauline. She shook her head in greeting, twiddled her fingers, banged her helmet with an open hand. Pauline, next to her, in her dress and the makeup I had so carefully applied that morning, looked, if anything, too normal for this place. Though I knew that looks, especially in her case, were always deceiving.

Pauline was silent as we left, the staff asking her if she wanted a snack. She refused to look us in the eyes, as if to prove some point, as if to say fuck you, which were exactly the right words.

The silence continued on the ride home. My father and I couldn't speak. Back at the house, uneasy, angry, I restarted my medication.

Chapter 13

Statistically, a girl who plays a varsity sport in high school will outearn a girl who doesn't by 30 percent in her lifetime. She is half as likely to have a child out of wedlock and one-third as likely to have a child while still in her teens. She will score higher on standardized tests, have a higher GPA, and also be twice as likely to graduate from a four-year college. She is far less likely to be prescribed antidepressant medication.

A female college athlete will outearn her nonathletic peers by $228,000 over the course of her working life. Her marriages will be more durable, her life expectancy longer. Her responses to survey questions about personal happiness at ages twenty-five, thirty, and thirty-five, which is as far as the studies have gone, will place her in a far higher percentile for general satisfaction. She is more likely to describe her relationships with her children as "stable" and "positive." She will be more self-confident. She will repay her student loans earlier. She is also far less likely to be on antidepressant medication at ages twenty-five, thirty, and thirty-five.

There have been no studies done as to how she will manage her rage and anger issues.

The women's national team was still the stepsister of the men's team. The United States Soccer Federation spent about a nickel on the girls for every dollar spent on the boys. But the women's gold-medal game in '96—a 2–1 US victory over China that hadn't even been televised but had sold out a football stadium in Athens, Georgia—had caught everyone's attention, men and women. One thing that game had proved: the boys didn't draw like the girls. Just look at America's youth leagues. Soccer, at least in the United States, was as much, or more, a girl's sport than a boy's. So the girls were now, finally, being allocated resources, and sponsors were ponying up, a decade after legislated athletic equality. We were nowhere near actual equality, but these minicamps, the Under-17 team, the residency for the national team, all of it was a big step for women's soccer.

I never saw playing as heroically standing up for a cause or being a feminist. I just wanted to play.

The spring minicamp at the University of Texas was the last time Coach Tony would see us before making decisions about whom to invite to the national team residency that summer. In practices I was controlled, calm, and patient, even with Alexis, my competition for the right offensive midfield. I never threw an elbow, barely shoved, kept my arms and hands low, was unselfish with the ball, and generally had that sense of the game coming to me. My feet were healthy, my mind sound. Dozens of college coaches trooped through practice, through the scrimmages against the UT varsity team, and finally through the friendly against China, in which I started and scored one goal for a 3–1 victory. I played consistent, lovely soccer, never drew a card, and in the dorms kept on good terms with the other girls, avoided Alexis, and made every effort to be sociable.

Coach Tony praised me in film sessions, calling out good decisions I'd made, even suggesting that I was the most improved player in the camp. Dr. Dorfman and Dr. Gifford took evident pride in me, as if I were a project that was working out. Dr. Gifford grinned with each measurement she took, and Dr. Dorfman nodded with each well-adjusted answer I fabricated.

I was striving to show that I'd matured, settled down, become capable of playing without violence—that I'd grown up. Was it all contrived? I didn't think so. Even without my meds, I was less quick to anger; I had resigned myself to internalizing my rages so that instead of throwing a punch or an elbow, I could take deep breaths, take up the right space on the field, and even, when I was fouled, look for the official instead of retaliating. I was doing what my therapist called acting my way into right thinking.

"You have a reputation," Dr. Dorfman had told me at our first session during minicamp. "The other girls think you rattle, lose your cool. Don't let them use that."

All of this seemed to surprise Alexis. She'd anticipated my hotheaded reactions and tried to provoke me in one-v.-ones and scrimmages. When I didn't respond to her hard challenges, her high tackles, she lost some of her edge. I imagined her recalculating, wondering how she could get me to lose my cool on the field the way I used to.

Where it mattered most, in front of every top college coach in the country, I demonstrated that what they'd heard about me—my tantrums, my violence, my fouling, my fighting—was in the past. What they saw was a beautiful player: the same player Brendan had fallen for, the same player you'd fall for if you saw me play. And when I capped in the Under-17 game against Japan by putting in a left-footed volley that even Fabien Barthez couldn't have stopped, I knew I'd just secured my ride to the college of my choice.

An invitation to residency was now a foregone conclusion. It was obvious to everyone who saw me at minicamp that I was among the twenty-one best players in the country. After those final days on the pitch, I looked in the mirror, and I saw the blood and dirt and sweat and grass. My own sweat a slick coat, my face drawn and thin from dehydration, my crooked nose a badge. I believed I'd indeed turned into a worthy person, good enough for the national team, pretty enough for Brendan. A girl could have a life in soccer, even in America, and we would be pioneers, role models even. You didn't have to have a supermodel body or a little button nose; you could be muscular, hipped, haunched, and broad, and still be fetching. Or so I started telling myself.

Chapter 14

My father and I visited Pauline every Thursday—my only day free from soccer—bringing her a carton of sweet-and-sour pork from Hops, some rice, and a guava lemonade, all of it from Fernando, for free. Pauline was always happy to see us, shooting her innocent, unrestrained smile, but then she'd remember how angry she was at us for abandoning her, and she would retreat back into her disappointment. She'd regressed in the group home; that was obvious to me. She was rocking more, was losing the words she'd had, and was even more distracted, if that was possible, than before.

When I showed her the clothes I'd brought her—a new pair of jeans, some shoes, a blouse—she'd become curious, happy again; but then, by the next Thursday, the item, if it was any good, would be missing. Everything of value, everything she loved, was taken. We complained to Sylvester, the Caribbean-accented bald man who oversaw the house for Found Horizons, that her clothes were being stolen, that her shoes were going missing, that her Walkman was gone, her hairbrush. He promised he'd look into it.

He told us that Pauline had a habit of growing agitated in the mornings, refusing to board the van to her new school. She'd even scratched one of the other students, which meant that the attendants had to duct-tape her into gardening gloves before her ride to school.

One Thursday we came and found a fresh scab inside a bruise in the dead center of her forehead. The house psych tech—that's what they called the twelve-dollar-an-hour staffers—on duty at the time of the incident had given her a Band-Aid and written it up as self-inflicted.

When the day psych tech came in, he saw the bleeding and sent Pauline to the emergency room.

As worrying as the incident was, it worried me more that Found Horizons had failed to call us to report the injury, a breach of every protocol. Sylvester apologized profusely for this mistake but said that otherwise the incident had been handled correctly. There was nothing they could do if some of the residents harmed themselves.

But Pauline hadn't hit herself in years, I reminded my father. That had been one of my father's great triumphs, getting Pauline to cut out self-destructive behavior.

My father saw it as regression, a natural result of the stress of her new location. I wondered whether that was all it was.

I spooned the sweet-and-sour pork into Pauline's mouth and let her have the bowl of rice, and when she was finished, I laid my forehead against the side of hers.

"I love you," I said. "Okay? I love you."

"H-h-h-h-home," she said. "T-t-t-t-take—"

I knew what she wanted. I told my father we needed to get her out of there, and he said he would talk to Sylvester, would seek a better situation.

Meanwhile, Found Horizons' medical staff suggested that Pauline receive stronger medications. "To cut down on the incidents of SIIs," a doctor said in a conference call with my father and Sylvester. SIIs were self-inflicted injuries, another acronym.

They increased Pauline's dosages of diazepam, Haldol, and Zyprexa. That made two of us on prescribed antipsychotic medications.

But I had Brendan, the beautiful man in my life, and for a few weeks, even knowing what Pauline was going through, I was able to lose myself in desire and the fulfillment of that desire. Brendan began spending his lunch periods—when he was at school—leaning into the brick wall next to the physical education offices, his long, lean body making a puddle of shade.

We were never going steady, not in the classical high school sense, but we were something—a curious item, an odd couple made possible by the fact that Brendan was so handsome and so popular that he didn't give a fuck what anybody thought.

At home, the window locks were all broken, the carpets were stained, and one of our boilers had crapped out, which meant no hot water in the rear bathroom. I would have been embarrassed to have anyone over if I'd had anyone to invite over. But all I had was Brendan.

I received a package in the mail inviting me to residency that summer, the live-in camp with the actual national team. If I performed well at residency, I would probably have a shot at the USWNT itself. I was so close.

And so was Alexis. I heard from Lorena that Alexis had gotten the same invitation.

Gwen, apparently, hadn't made it. Alexis and I wound down that school year without speaking, but I was sure we were dreaming the same dream.

Of the seven of us girls who'd been playing together since grammar school—the best seven girls in Los Angeles, arguably—two of us had made it to residency. That I was one of the two was maybe predictable, but that I was the one of the two kissing Brendan was remarkable.

The sun was shining on me, and in my happiness and joy I forgot my problems, my sister's problems. I forgot, for days at a time, my mother. What we had lost.

I attended a varsity volleyball game in which Brendan, our best middle, was playing. I stopped at the double doorway, under the lintel, reluctant to take a seat in the stands, wary of gossip. Half of my teammates weren't even talking to me because of Alexis. So I stood where I was, in the entryway, watching the match. I saw several of my teammates, but I didn't see Alexis. Brendan didn't know I was there. Would he have cared?

The longer I stood by the door, wearing a pair of sweats and a tank top, my feet in slides, my hair tied up, I could see that I had, in fact, become a part of something. Girls were pointing at me, were leaning into each other and looking my way. Most of our classmates paid no attention to the soccer team, so I knew my sudden renown had nothing to do with my success on the Under-17 team or the championship season the Sea Lionesses soccer team had just completed. It had to do with the fact that I had the most beautiful boy. Didn't that mean I rated highly as well?

That night, my father asked whether I was happy.

He was sitting in our living room, an early-season baseball game on television—the Dodgers were on the East Coast. He sat there with a 7 and 7 in his hand and his back turned to the game.

I didn't recall him ever asking me before. He said I seemed different, lighter somehow. It was easy for him to discern weightlessness, I supposed, because he was so heavy. Dragged down by his drinking, the gambling, the memories of his wife, and the disappointment of Pauline. He had felt buoyant only at sea or in the blissful tide of his marriage to my mother.

I couldn't tell him I was happy. That seemed somehow too simple an explanation, so I defaulted to "I'm the same."

"Maybe the medication's working," he speculated. I shrugged.

The way he financially engineered our lives—persistent and complex refinancings of our home, lines of credit at several banks as well as the ledger at Hops—was perhaps his greatest talent. He could frivol away evenings gambling on sports and cards yet never lose so much it hurt. He was something the Gamblers Anonymous folks would never admit existed: the degenerate noncompulsive gambler. He seldom bet enough to negatively impact our lives when he lost but also never had a spare $1,150 so I could attend Kyle Rote Jr.'s summer all-star camp. He lived in this murky no-man's-land of small bets, managed losses, and undaring expectations—a life spent middling, a bunch of low-stakes wagers that, even had they all come up losers, wouldn't have made a difference. As for winners? Those also wouldn't have mattered. It was a diversion in petty action, but it still left me nervous that he might suddenly get the idea that he was smarter than he was.

"Tonny would have been so proud," he said, using the nickname he'd always used for Mom. "National team. This camp you're going to. It's a real achievement. But would it kill you to read a book once in a while?"

He handed me a paperback of *Angela's Ashes*.

I wanted to give him credit, to praise him for all he'd done to support me, but I couldn't open my mouth. Sure, he'd driven me to Tri-County and regional games, he'd encouraged me, but he hadn't even had the money to pay for regional finals trips to Sacramento or San Diego, for flights to the ODP. The other girls' parents had to pay my damn NSCAA fee for last season. So did I really owe my father anything? Or had he just done the minimum?

I didn't want to start accusing him of disappointing me as a father, so I just nodded at him, his droopy, lidded eyes, his sleek, strong nose, and his thick lips. He was still a handsome man, but his looks were fading with the rest of him, his wispy dirty-blond hair thinning out, his stomach now bulging a little over his jeans. He gave off the sense that he had expected so much more but had ended up with this, with us, with me.

Or was I projecting?

No matter. I couldn't bring myself to compliment my father for his role in bringing me to this place, to the precipice of every girl's soccer dreams: to play for the national team, to go to college on a full ride. I couldn't tell him I loved him. I couldn't thank him for doing all he could do in a fucked-up situation. I was so stingy with my praise, my gratitude, my understanding.

But I was no harder on the rest of the world than I was on myself.

Chapter 15

The last Under-17 game before residency began was against Mexico, played in San Diego. We took them apart 7–1. Their team had only just met each other three days before the game, and most of them lacked the fitness of top American high school players. Their best players, actually, were the American girls of Mexican descent who'd come to our ODP camp, whom I'd eaten lunch with every day, who'd failed to make the American Under-17s. They'd found a home on the Mexican team based on having two Mexican grandparents, as was the requirement. Girls who failed to make the US team often rediscovered their heritage, returning to England, Ireland, Spain, or any of the other second-tier women's national teams to get a spot.

This was my best game yet as a national player, scoring a pair of goals before leaving the game with what turned out to be a broken nose at the fifty-eight-minute mark. I didn't even notice when it happened, but apparently I'd collided face-first with a Mexican defender's chin as I was going for the ball. I was on my back on the pitch for a few minutes, blood gushing through my hands as I tried to sit up and then was pushed back down by one of my teammates. Dr. Gifford came out onto the field, along with Coach Tony, and the two of them carefully sat me up, holding a towel under my nose.

I felt fine, just a little tingling at the bridge of my nose. "You're done," Coach Tony said.

"What? Fuck no," I said.

"True," Dr. Gifford said. "Your nose may have been broken. You can't take—"

"I can finish the game." I stood up, holding the towel to my face. I could see by my teammates' expressions that I must have looked awful.

I moved the towel away from my face and saw it was saturated with blood.

I began to walk off the pitch. There were cheers from the small crowd in the stands at Triton Stadium. The Mexican team actually had more supporters than we did, but that was pretty typical for American soccer games against Mexico in California. My dad was somewhere out there, and I waved as I walked off the field, along the sidelines, and then across the bleachers to the little blue tents where we had taped up before the game. My father walked over and stood nearby, conferring quietly with one of the assistant coaches. I sat in the shade with Dr. Gifford, who told me I was going to be fine, which I found strange because it never occurred to me that I wouldn't be fine.

A few minutes later, a paramedic arrived, and I wasn't allowed to walk to the van.

Instead, they brought a wheeled gurney over and made me lie down on it, and then they slid me into the van like a loaf going into an oven. Dr. Gifford said she'd follow in her car. I was aware of my father also saying he'd join us at the hospital.

As soon as we arrived, I was wheeled into a critical-care suite, a curtain was drawn to give me privacy, and the nurse told me to take off my uniform and slip into a hospital gown. After a few minutes, I was greeted by a Dr. Ghosh, who took away the bloody towel I was holding and then bent down to study my nose, which was now throbbing and sore to the touch.

"Can someone get me some sweats or something?" I asked Dr. Gifford, who'd arrived in the curtained-off emergency suite.

She said my father had some sweats for me. He'd be in in a minute. "But they want you to wear the hospital gown."

"We'll get you up to Radiology," Dr. Ghosh said. "We'll take an X-ray, and then we'll make a plan, okay?"

The bleeding had slowed, and I began to feel a little bit faint. I fell asleep for a few minutes and woke up when an orderly, an Asian woman with frizzy hair and teeth that seemed too large for her mouth, came in and wheeled me over to Radiology, where a woman named Alis-Alihajishik (I remember because she introduced herself as such, and in my state, I couldn't remember whether that was her first name or last name or both) asked me whether I was okay to sit up, and I said I was, and she slid a heavy lead-filled vest around my abdomen, fastened it at the back, put me in a chair, and then had me put my chin on this plastic rest. She left the room, and the camera began shooting my face, first from one side and then the other.

She came back in and slid me out of the apparatus and the vest. "Is it broken?" I asked.

"I take 'em." She shrugged. "I can't read 'em."

It was broken. After consulting with Dr. Gifford, Dr. Ghosh told me she would reset my nose but that it would be only a temporary resetting. The team would consult a cosmetic surgeon regarding the eventual reshaping of the nose, she promised. For now, it would be crooked, Dr. Gifford told me when my dad was in the room with us.

"It already is," I said.

"More so," Dr. Gifford said. "That's why we'll find you a cosmetic surgeon."

I shrugged. It hurt to open my mouth, so I talked through clenched teeth. "Can it be straightened?"

Dr. Gifford nodded. "The USSF has insurance. And your own insurance—"

My father nodded his head. "Medi-Cal."

"Well, there are options. The important thing is to do the temporary setting, stop the bleeding and the pain. You'll be in a mask for a few weeks."

"A mask?" I said. When I'd broken my nose in Tri-County, they'd set it in a little triangular plastic guard. The technology had apparently advanced. They had clear plastic masks with padding all around so that I could even play in a week or two. But I had to keep my nose stable and set in the mask.

They reset my nose, which made a sound like separating a drumstick from a thigh. I'd rejected the offer of pain medication and grunted my way through it, passing out once from the pain. Finally, on the drive back home, I took two Tylenol and drank a few slugs of a red sports drink, which tasted of the blood that had been in my throat. I slept on my side, my plastic face mask baking my flesh in the early-evening sun.

Coach Tony called me the next morning to say how pleased he was by how I was playing. "Right now, you're our leader," he said. "You're the girl who's setting the tone for our team. I couldn't be more pleased. You can choose where you want to go to college."

"National team?" I asked.

"Keep playing like this. Keep control like this. And yeah, I think that's the course you're on."

"Have you told Coach Dorrance?" I asked. Dorrance was the head of the national team.

"Dorrance is out," he said. "I'm taking over."

Despite my broken nose, despite having to wear a plastic plate for the last three weeks of school, I was elated. Coach Tony had basically told me I would make the national team. A full ride to college was a foregone conclusion. My transcripts were good enough anyway, and my soccer résumé could get me in anywhere I wanted. Where did I want to go? Duke? University of North Carolina? How about UCLA? Why not? It was close, so I could be near Pauline and my dad, and it was a great soccer school. This was the spring when it seemed like all my dreams would come true.

And I deserved that, right?

Chapter 16

Brendan didn't like the mask. He made it clear. He'd accepted me with my slightly crooked nose, even appreciated my muscular body, loved my powerful legs, but he just couldn't date a girl in a plastic mask. I understood. But couldn't he wait a few weeks? The mask would come off.

No. He wasn't a patient boy. Never had been. I guess being with me had been a 51-49 proposition anyway, so during those waning weeks of school, as the days lengthened so that the twilight felt like an entire day unto itself, a beginning, middle, and end, the gloaming as long as all that had come before, Brendan dropped me.

Brendan stopped coming around, left me to eat my lunch by myself, never called, never drove by, and I told myself it was to be expected, that he'd been a stroke of good luck. I didn't fight for him or pine; I let him go. What else could I do? I felt monstrous, the heat of my own flesh trapped inside the hard, clear shell, which, despite the ventilation holes, still came to smell of my own sweat and dead skin. I cleaned it as often as I could, un-Velcroing the mask, rinsing it, then reapplying it. But the smell leached into me, and I was reluctant to come too close to anyone. So I withdrew. I became even more invisible, my solitary lunch routine unchanged, making my way to the waning days of AP US History or Math Analysis, taking my seat, facing front, ignoring the sidelong looks and whispers. I had gone from dating Brendan Leaf, the cutest boy in the school, stud volleyball player, to being some sort of leper.

When my therapist asked about the mask, how I felt, I told her it didn't bother me. I didn't tell her that it had ruined my life, that one fucking broken nose had upset this wonderful balance that I'd found. I didn't tell her that I felt the change immediately when Brendan broke up with me—I clenched my jaw and moved to open space, as I did on the pitch. I told her the only thing that mattered was residency, was the national team, was my soccer. And in that world, I was fine. I'd started playing again just a few days after returning from the Mexico game.

And for my teammates, or most of them, there were only lesser soccer camps, summer leagues, various college application–burnishing activities, schools in England, and internships in Washington, DC. For the first time, I didn't begrudge any of them their fancy lives; I was on my own path, better than anyone else's. Make the national team this year, and then next year, I had a chance to be on the squad that would go to Three Nations, and then the Women's World Cup, where we could take revenge for the loss to Norway in '95. I could win a gold medal in Sydney—there were unlimited upsides. All because I maintained my discipline, ate my dry chicken, drank plenty of water, and outran, outworked, and outplayed every girl I came across. All because I wanted it more and tried harder. It started with my talent, I knew, but it would end only if I chose to give up. And I never fucking give up, not between the touchlines.

Of course, I wasn't really fine. It pained me more than ever to see Alexis, at school or on the pitch, because my own physical distortions made her seem even more perfect. If I had outplayed her in the Under-17s, she had outplayed me in life. She even had Brendan back. That handsome moron was so lacking in imagination that within a few days of my wearing the plastic mask, he was back to seeing Alexis.

The therapist asked about my medication. I looked at the poster on her wall, a map of the Milky Way with a "You Are Here" arrow pointing to the earth, and then at a needlepoint next to it of an elephant that said, "Life Is Beautiful." I lied and told her I was still taking my meds.

I didn't tell her that I'd stopped taking the meds weeks ago, even before my broken nose, that I felt they slowed me down, dulled my edge, that I needed my aggression and ferocity or I couldn't be an effective soccer player. Instead, I nodded, told her I felt less anxiety and anger, a greater sense of well-being. On a scale of one to ten, ten being the happiest, I was a fucking eleven, okay?

I wanted to tell her about Pauline, about the fucked-up group home, about the bruises she was getting, about how she cried when she saw us and begged us to take her home, about how unfair life was, that one of us could get to play on the national team while the other was stuck on the autistic team, and that even with all the goodwill in the world—and I believed there wasn't that much—her team was stuck at the bottom of the table. I wanted to tell her that nobody would ever love Pauline. That in a world where certain people get the bad breaks, not because they're bad people, but because they have bad brains, how do you maintain pretense that it's nothing but a shit show?

I had come to suspect that any complaints about life in general, or my own struggles or sadness, would be noted and then reported to Dr. Dorfman and then to Dr. Gifford and then to Coach Tony, and they would see that I hadn't actually changed at all, that I was as angry and prone to violence as ever. So I learned to tell a version of my life that sounded and felt like I was a normal, happy, well-adjusted soccer player. And I was, right?

I salvaged my usual Bs for the semester, got a 1 in AP US History, a 2 in AP Bio, and a 4 in AP Lit, but who cared? I wasn't getting into college based on my academics. Point Dynamo won our NSCAA regionals, and I was voted most valuable player by my teammates for the first time.

Alexis had always gotten that honor. So even though she remained the most popular player, my teammates had decided I was the best.

I finally removed my plastic mask a few days after school ended. The bridge of my nose had both flattened and widened, giving my face a smudged quality, a little like the drawings of early man in natural history textbooks. If you've seen Brando when he was young and beautiful in *On the Waterfront*, you've seen my nose. The overall effect made my face seem rounder, less sleek, and, I believed, almost simian.

I dreamed of having my sister's nose. As soon as I could, I called the cosmetic surgeon Dr. Gifford had recommended.

The receptionist said that before making an appointment, she had to remind me that the doctor didn't take any health insurance. I understood this to mean that his kind of sculpted, repaired noses weren't for people like me.

I was afraid to call Dr. Gifford or Coach Tony to ask them about my nose. I didn't want to do anything that might compromise my position on the team—and I didn't want to arrive at residency with another plastic face mask. So I lived with it, crooked, splayed. But none of it would matter if I made the national team.

Chapter 17

Without school or the NSCAA season, I had more time, and I drove the Celica down to Gardena whenever I could. One morning I dropped in on Pauline without calling ahead per Found Horizons' client policy. She was in her room wearing nothing but urine-stained panties and a torn T-shirt, her arms bruised, her pubic hair spilling out the top of her underwear. She smelled like pee. I knew Pauline was too vain to live like this; she'd become obsessed with makeup, with pretty clothes. As soon as she saw me, she hid her face between her knees and rocked back and forth.

When I tracked down George, the most senior psych tech on duty that morning, he was in the kitchen, drinking iced tea from a tall plastic glass. I confronted him. He said that Pauline had been acting out, scratching the psych techs, and that, as a negative reinforcer, they'd taken away her jeans and tops. She wouldn't get them back until she cooperated.

In the living room, two of the boys were banging their hands against the walls, making the windows rattle. Another boy was wearing a football helmet in the corner. Again I wondered, did Pauline belong here? These boys seemed more disturbed. Or was it my familiarity with Pauline that prevented me from seeing her as she actually was? A peer of these very fucked-up teens.

I returned to her bedroom and found that more of the clothes and makeup I'd given her had been stolen. I found a pair of old jeans and handed them to my sister.

"B-b-b-b-b-b-b-b-b-b," she said.

I nodded. "I know, Paul, bad boys."

She nodded, rocked back and forth. The bruises, the scab on her forehead looked fresh. I gave Pauline my hoodie and told George I was taking her out for lunch.

He asked how old I was. I told him I was seventeen.

"She can't leave with a minor," George said.

"What's your fucking malfunction?" I said, standing close to him. He had about five inches on me, but I connected with my old rage, the bad old me, and made a quick jerking motion with my head, as if to head-butt him, but I managed to check myself, stopping short. "I'm taking my sister to lunch."

George looked around, as if unsure of the proper procedure. He had me sign and date a piece of paper on a clipboard and then sort of shrugged.

I took Pauline out to the car and let her sit in the passenger seat, and she was so grateful at our little day trip that she didn't throw her shoes out the window as I drove around Gardena, looking for a crappy Chinese restaurant so that I could at least give Pauline a good dose of sweet-and-sour pork.

"T-t-t-t-t-take me—" Pauline said.

"I can't take you home," I said.

"P-p-p-p-p-p-p."

I found a strip-mall fast-food Chinese place called the Wok Inn and let Pauline out of the car. I led her into the restaurant, gathered trays, and loaded them with white rice and gooey orange-colored breaded pork, and then we sat down facing each other at a two-top with built-in hard plastic chairs.

She reached out to touch my nose. I flinched but held steady. She felt the still-tender bridge of my nose and squinted. "B-b-b-b-b-broken."

I nodded. "Sure is."

"B-b-b-b-b-boyfriend?" she asked.

I was surprised by her intuitive leap from my marred appearance to its effect on the opposite sex. She was more aware of the ways of the world than I sometimes gave her credit for.

I nodded. "Yes, I have a boyfriend. We're so happy." I forced a smile.

She blinked, chewed her orange pork, sipped her orange soda. I knew I wasn't supposed to let her have this much sugar, but then, what other pleasures did she have? Everything she loved, or even liked, was being systematically taken from her. After lunch, I wiped her mouth with a wet napkin and then asked for the lavatory key, leading Pauline into the bathroom, where she washed her hands.

After drying them with a towel, she laid her head against my shoulder. Her hair smelled awful.

I drove her back to our house, her first visit since we'd put her in Found Horizons, and a strictly AMA (against medical advice) leave, but I couldn't drive her back to the group home. She was bouncing up and down, despite my repeated warnings that this was just a visit. After a few minutes, I gave in and just let her enjoy the sensation of returning home. When we pulled up, she bounded from the car and then ran onto the lawn, where she sat down on the Spanish moss, picking up handfuls of the stuff, twiddling it around in her fingers. She turned to me, smiling.

I took her into the bathroom, ran a bubble bath, and dunked her in it, letting her luxuriate in the warm water, the peach-scented froth, before I washed her hair with basins of the bathwater and then rinsed her off. She cried when some soapy water ran into her eyes but then calmed and blinked it out, impressing me with her newfound resilience. When she was dry, I put her in a pair of my old jeans and a blouse I'd grown out of; sat her in front of the mirror on a stool; powdered her face; applied pink lipstick, some eye shadow, and blush; gelled her hair; and even hit it with some hair spray to tease it out a little. I masked her bruises with foundation, which made her arms look powdered-sugar white. By the end of our makeover, she looked like a member of an '80s hair-metal band, but Pauline loved the attention and the transformation, and she sat gazing at herself, admiring her reflection from different angles, before galloping out to the living room and lounging on the sofa, jumping up every couple minutes to return to the bathroom to look at herself.

I don't know whether Pauline saw this as some kind of audition, whether she was attempting to prove she could maintain the tranquility needed to convince my father to allow her back in the house. But if that was her strategy, it didn't work. That afternoon, when my father came home from another unsuccessful day, his happy surprise at seeing Pauline in the living room quickly turned into obvious concern. I had breached Found Horizons' protocol. She wasn't supposed to have a home visit for the first ninety days, we'd been told, to protect her from remembering all that she'd lost.

I apologized. I couldn't help it. I just couldn't bring her back to the group home.

He shrugged and immediately picked up the phone and called Sylvester, explaining that Pauline had been taken home by her sister, without parental approval.

Of course Pauline would be returning; I'd known that all along, but my father's stern adherence to the rules of a fucked-up place struck me as a betrayal. Whose side was he on?

"It's not us against them," he said to me.

"Clearly. It's me and Pauline against you," I said.

"No, it's all of us, in this together."

He was right. I would be going away in a few weeks. And then what? Pauline would be home alone?

But still . . . "That place isn't working."

"Maybe. But she's safer there than here on her own."

"You'll find another place?" I asked.

By now, Pauline was aware of the nature of our conversation and had become agitated, flipping over a coffee table in the living room, sending magazines sliding and an empty coffee mug bouncing off the carpet. She started pulling books and videocassettes off the shelves.

Unwittingly, she was proving my father's point—that we couldn't care for her at home anymore. "Paul," I said, "come on. It's okay. It's okay. I told you it was only a visit."

But she had willed herself into believing that she was home, and now the prospect of returning to the group home must have seemed like a revoked parole. In full makeup and a teased blowout, she bounced around the room, like a little Axl Rose throwing a backstage tantrum.

"Please, Paul," I said, risking getting close, trying to take her in my arms. She attempted to claw me once, but I was too fast, and I grabbed her and pulled her in, hugging her so tightly I felt her rib cage contract and the air rush out of her. I was strong, jacked up from triweekly weight-room sessions, and maybe I could squeeze the anger right out of her, squeeze out the malice, squeeze out the autism, squeeze her right back into being normal.

"Trudy," my father said. "Hey, True, let go. Let go. You're choking her."

Pauline had gone limp in my arms. I loosened my hold and led her over to the sofa, where she collapsed, gasping. I hadn't realized what I'd done.

My father drove her back to the Found Horizons group home that night.

"I'm going to take another crack at my novel," he said, as if to justify having returned Pauline.

I shrugged. Didn't care.

Two weeks later I flew to Orlando for residency.

Chapter 18

Residency was to be my great equalizer, proof that all those years of pay-to-play camps that I'd been unable to afford—and that Alexis had attended—didn't make as much difference as everyone believed. Despite my teammates' parents pooling their resources and paying for my travel and my team and uniform fees, they never paid for any individual skills-development programs, the expensive camps where MLS players and coaches helped players refine and hone their game. They wanted their daughters' teams to win; they didn't want me to be better than their daughters.

But I made do without those camps, because when I was sixteen, I found men's pickup soccer games. As soon as I could drive, I began to seek them out, traveling as far as East LA for a kickaround. It took some courage to walk onto a pitch of grown-ass men as a sixteen-year-old girl, but I managed. So while the other girls were playing against their peers, I was playing against Mexican gardeners, Russian immigrants, and UCLA frat boys, and I think those five-v.-fives helped me more than any camp would have. Or maybe I'm wrong. Maybe missing all those summers of regular coaching ultimately held me back?

No, it was never a matter of ability. Even Coach Tony would admit that. In terms of talent, feel, and touch, I was among the best players of my generation. But while the other girls spent their summers running institutional drills in the morning and painting their fingernails at night, I was learning the Italian, Russian, and Igbo for the word "foul."

I said goodbye to Pauline and flew to residency in Orlando, the ticket paid for by the USWNT. I had no idea when Alexis would be arriving. An assistant coach was waiting for me as I came down the Jetway, and then we walked over to another terminal, where we waited for Julie Monet to arrive.

I found it remarkable that Julie, a cocaptain of the USWNT, a veteran with dozens of caps, would now be on the same pitch as me, sleeping under the same roof. I'd been hearing about Julie for close to a decade, since she'd been at Mission Viejo High School and had been a Southern California Player of the Year three years running, when I was still playing biddy. She'd gone to Stanford, been a finalist for the Hermann Trophy, and then gone on to play on the national team that won the World Cup in 1991. She was an American women's soccer pioneer, and I knew, on some level, that I was here because of what she'd accomplished. But when she came down the Jetway, I was too shy to say anything—to thank her or even acknowledge that I knew who she was.

She carried a duffel bag and wore jeans, a hoodie, and a pair of running sneakers. We were the same height but of dissimilar builds. I was stockier at the back, with a lower center of gravity, and next to Julie, I felt like some kind of monster, huge and hideous while she was lithe and beautiful.

While the two of us and the assistant coach waited for another girl to arrive on a flight from Chicago, we sat in a row of hard-backed airport chairs attached at the base, an empty seat between Julie and me. Julie had long curly hair tied back into a short ponytail and wore a headband just over her forehead to keep hair out of her eyes as she flipped through a magazine.

It began to seem awkward, my not acknowledging her, our silence, considering we were prospective teammates and would be living together for the next six weeks.

"Um, I'm Trudy," I said. "This is my first, you know, residency."

She nodded. "Hi there."

I nodded. "So, I'm kind of nervous."

She looked up at me and smiled. "Nervous? You have no idea how easy you guys have it. A camp like this? Training table? Nutritionists? Masseuse? We lived on granola bars. You'll be fine."

And she went back to reading her magazine. I shrugged. *Well,* bitch, *whatever.*

We were staying in University of Central Florida dormitories, new players sharing rooms, while veteran players bunked alone. This was a college dorm, so besides the usual swag—the sweats, sneakers, energy bars, sports drinks, another new Discman from Sony—it was an austere environment. I was rooming with Amber from Tennessee, a lanky girl with large, beautiful feet who spent an hour every night giving herself a pedicure. They were so perfect—delicately arched with lovely, long toes and lacquered toenails that formed perfect half-moons—that I was embarrassed to take off my own sneakers. My feet were, as usual, mangled and bent, but they'd served me well so far.

Amber had been a *Parade* All-American in high school, and we'd played together in the Under-17 game against Sweden. She was a fast player who outran opponents, using her long legs to collect balls and then send disappointingly flat crosses into the box. Against average defenders, that worked, but I knew she could be easily frustrated if you bodied her so that she couldn't get clean runs. At this level, I suspected, she would either have to learn to play in the back, or she would have a short camp.

She greeted me with a big hug, which was how all of us Under-17 and ODP girls greeted each other, and as we reconnected with old teammates, the feeling was a little bit of us against them, the younger girls versus the USWNT veterans, the girls whose posters some of us had on our walls (not me—I had a Dennis Bergkamp poster on mine). These girls were our heroes, but here they were trying to hold us back.

We were all vying for the same twenty-one—or, really, if you wanted to start, eleven—spots on the national team. That was one way to look at it. Most girls were thinking of college as well. But if you were here, that meant you were also thinking of the World Cup, of the Olympics, of displacing one of those girls on the posters and taking a spot on the USWNT yourself.

At least I was. And so was Alexis.

By then, every girl knew that even though we hailed from the same high school, we weren't on good terms. During the check-in, when I met with Dr. Dorfman to talk about my therapy, my medication, and my "anger issues," as they called them, she asked why Alexis and I weren't getting along. She'd heard, I don't know from where, that we'd dated the same boy, though she didn't understand the chronology or outcome. She assumed that there was some jealousy, though on what side she said she wasn't sure.

"Look, she ended up with Brendan, so I don't think she'd be the one who is, you know, jealous," I told Dr. Dorfman.

"Jealousy will eat you up," Dr. Dorfman said.

I shrugged. "I'm not going to let that derail me. I can handle it."

"But does it still hurt you?"

"Hurt?"

"Thinking about them, about this boy being with Alexis. I'm thinking in terms of team chemistry."

"I won't let something like that screw with my chemistry."

"But the team—can you and Alexis coexist?"

"We don't have a choice."

"What we don't want, True, is more of the anger issues, the fighting, you know—"

"Me neither," I said. "I'm not going to let something like that get in the way of my dream."

"*Our* dream," Dr. Dorfman said.

"Right, *our* dream."

But when I walked down the hall, and there was Alexis walking toward me, I was unable to look up from the floor, to acknowledge her in any way.

That night, at our first team meeting, Coach Tony came in and greeted all forty of us, ranging in ages from seventeen to thirty-five, the best female soccer players in the United States.

"Take a look around," he ordered us. "Really take a look. You will be playing with, or against, each other for the rest of your football lives."

What he meant was that we would be teammates here at residency, on the Under-17 or Under-23 teams, or on the national team, or we would be playing against each other, in college or in professional leagues. We had to get to know each other, to respect each other, to communicate with each other, to support each other, even though we were competing against each other. Not all of us would make it to the national team, but we'd all represent our country at some level, and that would most likely be with some of the girls in this room.

"The pitch is 8,250 square yards," he said. "It's too big to play on without talking to each other. Without knowing who's in front of you, behind you, alongside you, without knowing where your sisters are. You're each a link, girl to girl to girl."

He said that we would go around the room, and we would all stand up and say our names and where we thought we could improve and what we wanted out of this residency. At first I expected forty platitudes, but very quickly, because Coach Tony had the veterans begin, it was clear that these women took this exercise seriously and were revealing truths about themselves to this room full of relative strangers. Some girls were specific: To keep focused and mentally in the game for all ninety-plus minutes. To make more first-time passes. To not shy away from contact. And others were more spiritual: To listen to teammates.

To try to help teammates. To not criticize teammates. Even to be better moms while at residency.

The '95 Women's World Cup team, most of whom were here in this room, had lost to Norway in the semifinals, the camera crews capturing the US women bitching at each other on the pitch while the Norwegians celebrated with a conga line on their knees. The American women quickly blamed each other, before coming together in Atlanta to win the first-ever Olympic gold medal for women's soccer.

When it was my turn, I said I wanted to play passionately but not violently. "I've had a problem with, I don't know, some call 'em cheap shots, but I think I'm just passionate and sometimes I get too aggro. I need to learn to play without that negative emotion coming up."

But as soon as I said it, I imagined my Under-17 teammates and the veterans sort of filing that fact away in their minds, that I could be rattled, could be made to lose my temper, that if it came down to it, if it was her against me for a spot, she might try to get me to lose my shit.

Or was I just being paranoid?

Dr. Gifford was pleased by my physical conditioning. She said my blood work was superb, my resting heart rate was an impressive fifty-six beats per minute, and my body-fat index was 13 percent. I'd even grown a half inch yet hadn't added any weight. My strength training had given me more upper-body definition. She asked why I'd never gotten my nose reset.

"Um, it didn't bother me," I said. "I sort of like my nose."

I didn't want to say it was because we didn't have the money.

Dr. Gifford read through something in my file. "The second time it's been broken."

She felt along the bridge, down along my nostrils, pressing against the septum. "It seems to have healed perfectly. And it does add some personality."

I liked to think so. I'd hated it at first, but now I felt it had the strange effect of making me prettier somehow, as if the obvious imperfection diverted attention from my other imperfections.

Then she smiled. "You have a chest now!"

She closed my file and looked at me. She must have gotten contact lenses; she wasn't wearing glasses. "You've come a long way, Trudy, from your first ODP."

I nodded.

"How are things at home?"

I shrugged.

"With your sister?"

I didn't like to think about Pauline, not while I was here. I shrugged again. "Okay, I mean, it's not a situation that ever goes away."

"Your father, he's able to handle it?"

I nodded. "Yeah."

"So you can focus while you're here?"

"I think so."

Chapter 19

Hot metallic-tasting air greeted us the next morning. After taping and dressing, we marched out of the training room and then down the long concrete tunnel to a newly shorn field, our cleats making that bass grumble on the asphalt. The sky above us pressed down with what looked like an impending storm but was actually, I was told, just typical Florida weather. There were cones set up along the sideline, and we collected balls and began dribbling between them, making easy turns and then coming back, before a few of us broke off to do one-touch passing drills, twenty right-footed and then twenty left, while the assistant coaches walked between the pairs of girls, checking in with each of us.

Then we did one ball in and turned, then followed the ball back out, and then dribbled around and then passed back in, a communication drill, which meant we had to quickly learn each other's names, because there were forty of us and forty balls, so as soon as we released a ball, one would be coming at us; if we didn't talk to each other and say to whom we were passing, the drill would degenerate into chaos, like a swarm of ants on a Tootsie Roll. But we had a purpose—to pass, catch, dribble, pass, catch, dribble—and Coach Tony stopped us when too many girls were off chasing loose balls or trying to carry two balls when some players were running around with none.

"You see?" he said. "If you don't talk to each other—shout, whistle, bark, I don't care. But if you're not communicating, when it goes silent, like it just did there, then it falls apart."

And we would start again.

Then came an afternoon of eight-hundreds, six apiece, before core and lower-body work with strength trainers and then finally, after nearly three hours in the Florida sun and another in the weight room, our first scrimmages, five-v.-fives, with no goalies, games to 3, four games of ten players each. These were my first opportunities to get runs in with members of the national team. I was on a team with Joy, which psyched me out at first. I was too deferential; she was nearly thirty, a gold medalist with dozens of caps. And she was more familiar with a few of the other girls, Under-23 players who'd scrimmaged with the national team before. I wasn't getting many touches, and when I did get the ball, it was in bad spots where Joy or one of the other girls was looking for help, leaving me alone with one or two players bearing down on me. But when they saw that I could handle these one-v.-twos and that I could either split the defenders or make a good clearance pass to safety, they showed more confidence in me and integrated me more completely into the side. This was an important test, because after a few initial indecisive plays, I quickly found my role and identity within our little five-girl squad—I was the central defender, and soon I was moving forward, handling the ball more than anyone else on the squad, including Joy. I'm not even sure she noticed, but she'd fallen into a more defensive position, deferring to me, which was almost unheard of for a player of her stature. But the other players noticed, and even Coach Tony wandered over to watch our scrimmage for a few minutes, his sunglasses bobbing up and down as he noticed. I was having a good first day.

That night, as Amber buffed her soles and then painted her nails, the rotten-fruit odor of the acetone making my nostrils itch, she talked about playing with the national team girls, how intimidating that had been and how she had never really felt comfortable. I nodded and agreed but thought to myself that I'd never been more comfortable.

As rezzies went on, that feeling only intensified. There was no drill or game situation or run or fitness that wrong-footed me. It was as if I'd been waiting for this camp my whole life, a place where there were great soccer players and the only thing that mattered was how well I played, not how well I got along with the other girls. Perhaps that did matter, but only on the pitch—or that's how it seemed. At this level, game and only game mattered.

I'd learned every girl's name, could summon their attention on the pitch, and Coach Tony had seen how quick I was to look for a good pass, an open teammate, to locate space on the field and make sure to direct possession that way.

But off the pitch, in the dorms after practice—after video sessions during which Coach Tony and the assistant coaches would break down that day's play, calling out good plays, dressing us down for mistakes or lapses in attention—while the other girls were watching videotapes of *Scream* or *Jerry Maguire*, I was in my room, uninvited to the little slumber parties. After a couple of nights, Amber was gone, too, watching movies with the other girls.

The heat meant I went through a liter of water every hour, but I never stopped to sip water until the coaches gave their signal. I waited the full half a match, forty-five minutes, plus injury time, before grabbing a drink, which meant I trained my body to go without water, even in 98-degree heat and 99 percent humidity, under blistering sun that would make a caiman's blood boil. Girls passed out, their skin turning bright red and then ghostly white as their kidneys started to shut down. Cramps were so common that we learned to play through them, literally running through the pain. The funny thing about leg cramps is that you feel them most acutely when you're badly beaten, when a player dribbles you so that you turn unnaturally in reaction, your legs tangled, your calves torqued in an awkward position. That's when a cramp squeezes your leg like a vise: your muscles roll under your skin as if a snake is coiling its way up your fibula, the pain so great that even though you know it will count against you, you writhe in agony on the turf, counting the seconds you're down, like a boxer, straining to get up before ten lest the coach subs you out and puts in a presumably stronger player.

The national team girls—Mia or Julie or Michelle or Brandi or Joy or Carla—could afford to nurse their cramps, ice them even during practice, alternate hot compresses and ice packs; they didn't have to play through them the way the rest of us did. I never asked for treatment during practice, never waved over a trainer, never took a sip of water unless the coach told us to.

I lost five pounds in five days.

Three girls went home that first week. They claimed they were injured, but we were all injured. We were all best described by the collection of body parts that were damaged, strained, pulled, separated, torn, contused, and bulging. The point of rezzies, as had been the point of the ODP, was to push us and see who broke.

Right—there were masseuses available. But they were booked until one in the morning by the national team girls. I never got a slot. Dr. Gifford gave me some tramadol, some Norco, some Baclofen, and extra potassium, magnesium, and salt tablets. She also asked whether I had enough of my antidepressant medication, and I told her yes, I was well stocked.

I hadn't even brought it with me.

The big girls never really accepted me, but they came to respect me. How could they not?

I was finishing first or second in fitness every day. I never dogged it in drills. And in scrimmages, girls who'd already finished their games made it a point to come and watch my game.

When the coach had the younger girls play the national team, whether in five-v.-fives or against the full squad, only two of us were competitive with the big girls: Alexis and, of course, me.

I had to admit it: Alexis was having an excellent rezzie. She was playing forward instead of midfield, and she seemed to have picked up a step, outrunning even some of the national team defenders, giving Joy and Carla matchup problems when Coach Tony had her playing the role of the Chinese striker Sun Wen or the fleet-footed Brazilian Marta in practices.

I didn't have Alexis's speed up front, but I was making my mark directing the attack, and when we scrimmaged against the national team, I was even getting Alexis the ball in what I knew were her favorite spots. And while Coach Tony and everyone else made sure to praise me for building up the attack and for my service, Alexis never once pointed to me after a goal.

But so what, right? I didn't care.

The bigger problem that I foresaw was that the only openings on the big team were in midfield, and Alexis could easily slide back, and there she would be, competing directly against me.

Politically, Alexis had already made sure to build alliances with the girls who mattered, with Michelle, Mia, Brandi, and Briana. These were the girls who formed the core of the national team, and with whom I'd rarely ever shared a word off the pitch.

Chapter 20

It was the eighth day of camp, and in two more days, we would break for a week so the USWNT could go to the Three Nations tournament. Some of the girls would be shipping off to represent the United States in Jamaica for a CONCACAF Under-23 tournament, and those found wanting would be sitting around, resting and recharging until the camp regrouped, spending the whole week reflecting on how they hadn't been good enough to make the Under-23s.

When I saw Coach Tony's Under-23 roster on the training room wall, I was broken. I hadn't made it.

Alexis was on the list.

I realized I hadn't cried in months. I was so used to hiding my anger that I took for granted I had to hide my disappointment. So I swallowed, blinked, and turned to walk back to my room, skirting a crowd of girls who had gathered around another list that was being posted by an assistant coach: players who would be traveling with the national team to the Netherlands for the Three Nations tournament. I leaned in, squinting, and was stunned to see my name way down on the bottom as the first alternate. I wasn't among the twenty-one official members of the team, but I would be traveling and practicing with the actual United States Women's National Team, and if anyone was injured or carded out of the tournament, I would take her spot.

This would be my first trip outside the United States, and Coach Tony and the United States Soccer Federation pulled some strings to get me my passport in just twenty-four hours. I'd barely brought anything to rezzies, just my kit, my shoes, and a few outfits, and when we were issued the national team travel guidelines, I was surprised to learn we were supposed to travel in skirts or dresses. I hadn't brought a skirt.

During a session with Dr. Dorfman, I was more stolid than usual until I finally admitted what was bothering me: I didn't have a travel outfit.

The other girls, I blurted out, would all have skirts or dresses, and all I had were jeans.

Dr. Dorfman smiled and said she would talk to Coach Tony and Dr. Gifford to see whether they could free up some budget for me so I could dress to the travel code.

The last afternoon before our departure, as I was coming in from the practice pitch, dousing my head with cold water from a squirt bottle, I saw Dr. Gifford sitting in a golf cart, leaning forward over the steering wheel.

"True," she shouted as I walked past.

I stopped.

"Shower up," she said. "We're going shopping."

I showered and changed into blue USWNT sweats, and Dr. Gifford drove me in her little two-seat Mazda roadster to an outlet mall somewhere between Orlando and Tampa, a horseshoe-shaped complex around a vast parking lot. The USWNT had found some room in the budget for me, and as we went through Banana Republic, Abercrombie & Fitch, PacSun, Brooks Brothers, and DKNY, the salesgirls pointed at my national team sweats, and Dr. Gifford confirmed that yes, I was a member of the USWNT, which wasn't true, technically. They brought over black dresses, floral dresses, and these lightweight wool skirt-and-jacket business-lady outfits, and I tried them on, one by one, and for the first time maybe ever, I wasn't embarrassed at how I looked in the mirror, but actually proud. I spun around, watching the hems billow, studying my calves, my shoulders, my waist, my neck.

I had always looked healthy, strong, but had so often swaddled my muscles, my physique, beneath layers of sweats and warm-up jackets, or maybe jeans if I felt dressy. I'd come to dislike how I looked in fancy clothes. Now, in my DKNY jacket and skirt, I felt like the girl I could have been if things had been different, and I had to restrain myself from bounding around the room like Pauline after a makeover.

Dr. Gifford waited outside the dressing room in her own version of these kinds of clothes: the black boots, the silver-gray skirt, the white blouse, the pearls. She was so pretty, I deferred all decisions to her. And in the end, she helped me purchase a pair of outfits—a black dress and a skirt-and-jacket combo—and a pair of black heels that went with both.

After an hour at the outlet mall, Dr. Gifford took me to an Italian restaurant that was part of a big hotel, convention center, and golf course complex. We found a table amid men in suits and some bros in sports jerseys; I ordered chicken and roasted vegetables, and Dr. Gifford ordered pasta with mushrooms and some wine.

"You're going to be the youngest player traveling," she said. "Are you going to be all right?"

I nodded. I didn't recall any adult being this concerned about me, well, ever. Besides my father. I focused on my chicken, cutting it into smaller and smaller pieces.

"I'm fine," I said, chewing my chicken.

"You're fine when you're playing," Dr. Gifford said. "Off the pitch . . ."

I shrugged. "Doesn't matter."

"It does, True. It does. You can't always be on the pitch."

I drank my water. It seemed strange to me, this woman overtly caring about me, this desire she had to impart lessons, to teach me. I wasn't used to being mothered.

She explained she would be traveling with us, would be there for me the whole time if I needed her. She ordered another glass of wine, and I waited while she finished it, talking about Maastricht, about how exciting it was to go overseas for the first time. And about her own career playing soccer at Virginia before going to medical school.

"Were you any good?" I asked.

She smiled. "Not like you, True. Not like you."

Chapter 21

We flew from Tampa to Miami, and then from Miami to Amsterdam. Most of us were seated in economy, but there were a dozen business-class seats as well, some of which went to Coach Tony, Dr. Gifford, and the USSF officials on the trip, which left a couple free for team members, and these were allocated to the captains—Mia, Julie, and Michelle—and then on a rotating basis by seniority. I was stuffed in the back, in my skirt and jacket, along with a third goalie, Tricia, who was also an alternate. She was a tall girl with short arms for a goalie but long, stalky legs that encroached upon my space. We'd hardly interacted in rezzies, but in Maastricht, we were going to be roommates. In her lap she had a bottle of water and a stick of roll-on deodorant, which she applied liberally during the flight, reaching under her blouse and rubbing on more. I didn't detect any body odor, so I assumed she was just taking every precaution.

Her parents had driven down to the Tampa International Airport to wave her off, as had some of the other national team players' parents and family members, many of whom would be making their way to Maastricht themselves for the tournament. Needless to say, my dad was not among them.

—

Our hotel in Amsterdam was the Kempinski, and despite the five stars in the window, it had a shabby lobby with worn, soft chairs, a narrow restaurant, no swimming pool, and no grand circular driveway, as I had somehow been imagining. Instead, the sliding glass doors of the hotel opened right onto a cobblestoned alley, which ran down to the broad square in front of the royal palace, where money changers gathered all around and trucks sold herring along one side.

The city that I saw from the bus windows reminded me of something from a Dickens novel I'd read in AP Lit, only with women on bicycles: long, thin alleys, tiny storefronts, men in caps, wooden casks on trucks, beer kegs being rolled down planks into basements below pubs.

We stayed there overnight and then took the air-conditioned bus down to Maastricht, swaddling ourselves in sweaters to stay warm. The USWNT girls, coaches, and USSF officials were checked into a Holiday Inn while the alternates and a few assistants were relegated to a pension about a kilometer away, closer to the train station. Because we were alternates, tournament rules said we couldn't stay with the team or even eat with the team. So it was Tricia and me and her deodorant crammed into a narrow room with beds that had creaky springs and wrought-iron black corner posts that stuck up in the shape of spades. The mattresses were thin, and we sank into them, the sharp springs pressing into our backs.

We had a slit window that opened onto a narrow street, giving us a view of a row of white buildings with mansard roofs that ended at Maastricht station. There was a persistent racket of mopeds and scooters, occasional cloudbursts of harsh, heavy rain. We were given a per diem of thirty-five guilders, about twenty bucks, and when Tricia and I went out that afternoon, we stopped in a supermarket, and I saw that I could buy eighteen chicken breasts with that money, if only I could find a way to cook them, but Tricia insisted we go to a proper restaurant, and she spent her entire per diem on lobster bisque and french fries. I ate the bread rolls and drank some coffee.

After that we walked down to the Holiday Inn and rode the bus with the rest of the team to the De Geusselt, where some of the group games would be played and where we were going to have a light practice. The Three Nations tournament was put on every four years by the Netherlands, Germany, and Belgium, and was staggered to fall in the off years between the Olympics and the Women's World Cup. It was a major women's soccer tournament, but it wasn't one that you dreamed of playing in when you were a kid. I'll put it this way: it wasn't even on TV in the States.

Coach Tony dispatched a junior trainer, a San Jose State University assistant coach named Tyler, who had played one season in Britain's Second Division, to work with Tricia and me apart from the national team. According to tournament regulations, we couldn't even work out with the team, so this meant a dreary, drizzling afternoon of fitness, cone dribbling, and one-touch passing, and then we watched the big girls scrimmage until it was time to break. At least we could share the bus back to the Holiday Inn. By the time we got back that first day, Tricia's parents had arrived and booked a suite for her family at the Holiday Inn as well, so that meant I returned to the pension by myself, stopping at a market that had rotisserie chickens turning on spits facing a wall of red coils, the operation looking a little like a foosball table stood on its end. I bought a chicken, a bottle of water, and some spinach. I washed the spinach in my sink, doused it with bottled water, and then ate it raw. Then I ate all the white meat on the chicken and tossed out the fat and dark meat. Then I couldn't get to sleep because of jet lag, so I wandered around Maastricht, walking down the deserted streets and crossing the bridge over the river, where a few cutters and houseboats bobbed against the lichen-streaked stone banks. I thought of my father and his dream of buying a new boat, his fantasy about going back on the water, and I realized it was his idea of escape, his fantasy. He'd never buy another Hobie Cat.

My escape was here, right now.

There were a few bums by the water, older men huddled in groups or seated with their backs to the masonry walls along the riverbank. I walked past some large stone fortifications and down more dark streets, passing dozens of boutiques closed for the night, and then to a large square on which cafés had their tables set up and waitresses with heavy coin purses attached to their belts took orders and made change. I still had a few guilders of my per diem, so I ordered a Coke and drank it opposite a church whose massive stone steeple was lit from beneath. The rain started again, needle-sharp little droplets that stung my face, so I slid under a canopy and waited it out before walking back up to my pension, which turned out to be much farther than I had recalled. I rang the bell, was buzzed in, and went up to my bed, where I still couldn't sleep. I lay in my bed awake until light crept in and the mopeds and scooters started again, and then I finally dozed, and then there was a knock at my door, my wake-up call, and I dressed, grabbed my kit, forced down some Balance Bars, and got in a taxi with Tyler. Together, we rode back down to the Holiday Inn, met up with the other girls, and boarded the bus to De Krom stadium, where the team would play its first group match, against Finland. It turned out to be a warm afternoon, and those long, dehydrating training sessions in Orlando had left our girls better conditioned for this weather than the Finns, who looked ragged after they let in a pair of goals; they were clearly beaten and hardly mounted an attack after that.

The US team had a similar run against China, taking our rivals down 4–1 in a game played at the Stade Maurice Dufrasne in Liège, Belgium. But then, against the Norwegians, the same team that had beaten us at the Women's World Cup in '95, we fell apart, giving up a brace to Pettersen and one goal each to Riise and Lehn. The game ended in a 1–4 loss in Aachen, Germany.

Still, despite the loss, six points put us through to the knockout stage, the quarterfinal, which was played at the Parkstad Limburg, a twenty-thousand-seat Dutch First Division stadium, which was filled to capacity because we were playing France. We took them apart, 3–0.

I was a spectator for all of this, sitting in the stands with Tricia and her family, surrounded by crowds of Dutch, Belgian, and German fans. I wish I could say I watched these games with some pride or sense of camaraderie, but actually, all I really wanted was for someone to tire, lose focus, embarrass themselves—anything to give me an opening to step in. The first halves of the games I studied with some intensity, gauging my own abilities against what I saw on the field. And once I determined that I could play with, say, the Chinese or the French, then I began to lose focus, because the truth was that while I wanted the United States to win, I so desperately wanted to play that I couldn't bring myself to find goodwill for players who were blocking me from the national team. Brandi, Tiffany, Michelle, Julie, Kristine. If I were honest with myself, I wanted them to fail, even in knockout-stage games, where their failure might have meant the US team went out early. I felt ashamed at my own thoughts, sitting in those misty, damp stadiums. But the shame I felt at being a bad teammate was far outweighed by my desire to play.

There was no one for me to talk to about these feelings. I couldn't share them with Dr. Gifford or Dr. Dorfman; anything but full support for my team would have been seen as an obvious failing on my part, further confirmation of whatever diagnosis they'd slapped on me. And Dr. Gifford had just started believing in me. How could I compromise that?

But doesn't every elite athlete want her teammates to fail, at least until she's in the lineup and an actual part of the team? That's the unique tension of being an alternate. I imagined every alternate must have felt it, but when I looked over at Tricia, who was happily eating waffles and sitting beside her parents, all of them decked out in red, white, and blue and cheering giddily for the USA, I felt there must indeed be something wrong with me.

They gave us complimentary MCI phone cards that we could use to the call the States, and I called my father each night, his early afternoon, to see how Pauline was doing. The news was never good, but he told me she was hanging in there.

"Have you been to see her?" I asked.

He assured me he had, but I had doubts. I asked him how Found Horizons had responded to my taking her out for lunch and then back home, all of it illegal because I was still a minor.

"How's the tournament?" he asked without answering.

Chapter 22

In the semifinal against Germany, played in a nasty downpour that turned the field to slop, the big girls were cramping up badly in the cool air and suffering pulled muscles in the treacherous terrain. They had their worst game, losing 0–4, and we finished the game down three midfielders.

Coach Tony sat me down at the Holiday Inn that night, in the restaurant with blue bench seats on one side of the dining tables and wooden chairs with wicker seats on the other. He was drinking a beer, sitting with Tyler, the junior trainer from San Jose State, and Dr. Gifford, and they had evidently been discussing me, because when I sat down, Coach Tony turned to me and smiled.

"Are you ready?" he asked.

I nodded.

"We've decided to rest Brandi, Tiffany, and Michelle, and Julie is hurt. You're going to start in midfield against Japan."

The big girls didn't care about the third-place game, I knew. They hated consolation games, unless they were for an Olympic medal, maybe. But third place in Three Nations? Nobody really gave a shit. Except me.

I looked at Dr. Gifford, who gave me a slight nod and winked. "You're ready."

I pumped my fist once, but then quickly put it down beneath the table; I didn't want Coach to think I was exulting in my teammates' injuries.

"True," Coach Tony said. "This is an honor, to get your first cap before you're eighteen. It's rare, but you've earned it with a great residence and terrific soccer in the Under-17s."

I nodded.

This was the happiest moment of my life. I was told to go back to the pension and gather my gear, because I was now racking with the United States Women's National Team.

At practice, the big girls didn't seem surprised to see me. They'd watched girls come and go, I supposed, and they'd all once had their first caps as well. Which suited me, as I didn't want to attract undue attention. During fitness, I made sure to never challenge the top girls, and during scrimmages, I was a little tight, worried about making a mistake, until Coach Tony called me over and said, "True, I didn't promote you because of your good manners."

After that, I played ferociously, until Kristine pulled me over and said to save something for the game.

We played at the Rheinstadion in Düsseldorf in the afternoon, before the championship game, which was to be played that night. The huge stadium seated fifty thousand, but there were maybe five thousand in attendance, most of them Japanese. Third-place games didn't draw.

But to me, this was a signal moment in a life devoted to soccer—running out into that huge stadium, taking my place on the pitch, and playing for the national team. I wished Pauline could have been there to see me, and while I willed myself to remember every moment so I could tell her about it, I also knew I had to banish her from my head.

She was a distraction. I loved soccer because I didn't have to think of my sister when I was playing.

My first goal came on a lucky chance. Mia had found a little spit of space in the box and fired; the Japanese goalie, Onodera, made a lunging save that dribbled the ball out to Yamaki, who made a lazy clearance that I gobbled up just outside the box and fired right-footed at the lower-left corner.

1–0.

My second came just after halftime, and this was a thing of beauty. I put a long ball through to the right side, where Shannon ran under the pass and then poked it back inside to me. The ball was behind me, but I dragged it with my right foot so that it went behind my left leg, leaving Yamaki (again!) badly out of position. She swiped at me, but I was past her. It was a lovely move, done at pace, followed by a tap to the right that beat Nagadome. The shot was hard and rising, just past the diving keeper. This was the goal that my teammates would later tell me was the sickest goal in the Three Nations.

I deserved both those goals. They were each earned, because of how integral I was throughout the game in building up the attack, directing so much of our game from the midfield, even waving off some of the big girls or pointing to where I wanted them on the pitch. None of them seemed to resent it, as I was getting balls to girls in good spots.

I was comfortable throughout, and by the time Coach Tony took me off after seventy-five minutes to bring in another defender, I had completely forgotten where I was, I was so caught up in the flow. I took a seat at the far end of the bench, slapping hands with the girls all the way down, and finally, after I was handed a squirt bottle of water and a towel, I could contemplate what I'd done. I'd put in a brace for the national team, solidifying my chances to make that team, not just the Under-23s, but the actual frickin' national team, before the '99 World Cup.

After the game, in the locker room, Dr. Gifford came down and gave me a huge hug, and even Mia, Michelle, and the rest of the big girls, the veterans, each gave me a hug, too. They probably realized that this annoying and taciturn bitch who'd been giving them hell in rezzies was the real thing, and I wasn't going anywhere.

The Under-23s hadn't fared well in Jamaica. But Alexis had a terrific tournament, it turned out, playing almost every minute and scoring in five of six games. Once we were back in Orlando, the big girls were given a few days off to see family and friends, and Coach Tony told me I could return home if I wanted, as I'd earned a little vacay because of my play in Three Nations, but I told him I'd rather stay on here in Orlando and continue practicing with the girls. For the next five days, we had light fitness and afternoon scrimmages, the damp heat shocking after the Netherlands. Amber, my initial roommate at rezzies, was gone. She'd already been sent home after barely playing in Jamaica.

In her place was a brunette named Hunter, a junior at Wake Forest who also played midfield.

This was her second invitation to rezzies—she'd been an alternate this time—and when she arrived, she was courteous but guarded. We were battling for the same spot, of course, and she had already been briefed by Dr. Gifford on her roommate: me. It must have galled her, I imagined, for a high school girl to have already edged out a college junior on the depth chart, but these rankings were ephemeral, and a lousy next few weeks could knock me back down to the Under-17s, for all we knew.

The other girls who hadn't been to Three Nations were careful to let me know that they considered my performance to be asterisked, because it had been in a third-place game instead of group or elimination. I felt like telling them, *You try to score against fucking Japan—the best, most methodical defense in the world.* But instead I kept to myself, even avoiding my roommate, spending time in the video room, watching scrimmage and game footage, or in the training facility, doing upper-body weights and crunches.

Alexis had emerged as the leader of this junior contingent of girls, the girls trying to make the team, and I supposed that still included me, though I considered myself beyond them now. I was sure that I would continue to get called up to the USWNT now that I'd proved I could score at the highest level.

When the big girls returned to camp after five days, two-a-days started in earnest again, the usual routine of fitness, cones, ball drills, touch drills, communication drills, then scrimmages, different groups of five every day.

My confidence buoyed by my performance in Düsseldorf, I asserted myself in most game and scrimmage situations, challenging some of the USWNT mainstays and even prompting Coach Tony to pull me aside and ask me to dial it down. "You're coming off a little bitchy."

College coaches were now allowed into rezzies for some of the scrimmages. Dozens of them came and sat in the bleachers by the first mini-pitch, which became the scrimmage spot where Coach Tony put most of the Under-17s. They weren't allowed to talk to us, but I knew they knew who I was, because I'd already had a cap and a pair of international goals.

Dr. Gifford told me she'd had inquiries from almost every Division I program, asking for my medical report. "They're all interested."

Alexis, I already knew, was considering North Carolina, Wake Forest, and Stanford, three of the best soccer schools in the country. I'd taken my first SATs that spring and scored a disappointing 1,080 out of 1,600, which wouldn't have gotten me very far without a soccer scholarship, which was now virtually assured at the college of my choice.

"Where do you want to go?" Dr. Gifford asked me. "Wake? Stanford? North Carolina? UCLA?"

But during practice, Alexis continued to push for what I now saw as my spot. If the national team carried eight midfielders, I believed I would be the eighth and final, beating out my new roommate, Hunter, and, of course, Alexis. I'd proven myself in scrimmages and in national team play, but here at rezzies, Alexis was still a threat. She'd also proven herself, and she'd actually been more central to her team over a longer stretch with her performance in Jamaica. For years I'd heard that Alexis's game was more adaptable than mine, that she could fit into any formation, a 4-4-2, 4-3-3, whatever, but that was primarily because she was a longer, leaner player than I was. People have a hard time seeing past my body shape—boxy—so they underestimate my speed.

My stride is shorter, but I'm game fast, almost as quick as Alexis to any spot on the pitch. And soon, as Coach Tony made sure to put us on opposite sides in scrimmages, we were back to our old battles, each of us pushing the other. But there was no grudging respect, just contempt.

We'd been playing together for so long, since we were seven, and we'd been friends for almost all of the decade since. It was only in the last year or so that we'd become rivals, and then Brendan had severed any last ligaments of civility.

I tried not to distract myself with thoughts of Pauline—or my mother—but then I'd catch myself thinking of Brendan. I missed him, or, actually, I missed his body. Alexis and I both knew she'd won that game, and she reminded me of her victory whenever we happened to be in the same patch of the pitch. "Bitch," she would say. "Slut."

I tried to ignore her. But I knew she'd told everyone, the new girls, even the big girls, that I'd tried to steal her boyfriend. I wanted to stand up and address the team about the exact nature of this particular triangle, but how? How could I explain that it hadn't been theft? That they'd been broken up? That he had come on to me? Who could have chosen me over Alexis? Nobody would have believed me.

So I was left to play it out on the pitch, in daily scrimmages witnessed by some of the top college coaches in America. I admit, Alexis deserved some credit: she never conceded despite my higher perch on the depth chart, and she was playing her best soccer ever. But I was wearing her down. I knew she hated physical play—sharp elbows, a body against hers as she ran, the occasional hard foul—so I went all out. And because we were fighting for a spot, the assistant coaches let us play, swallowing some whistles to see who was the tougher of the two of us.

"Bitch," Alexis would hiss.

"Damn right," I'd snap back.

At night, my legs sore, my feet shredded, and my knees swollen, I'd sleep the beautiful, sound sleep of the honestly exhausted, waking with a headache halfway through the night and downing a half liter of water before falling back asleep. I was close, I knew, to breaking her.

What was one more day of pain and suffering, of hard running and mouthfuls of turf, of rough tackles and a bruised body? I could keep doing this until she dropped.

Chapter 23

My father was on the hallway pay phone. Pauline was in the hospital. She was fine, or she would be fine, but the police were investigating the exact circumstances.

"What circumstances?" I asked.

She'd been assaulted, he told me.

What the hell did that mean? "You mean like one of those guys with the football helmets hit her?"

"We're not sure." He paused. "Her jaw seems to be, um, fractured, dislocated. Both eyes are black. Another client, they're saying, beat her up."

"Where the fuck was the staff?"

"It's not clear. Nothing is. I'll call you when I know more. I'm going to the hospital now."

I felt my eyes starting to run right there in the pay phone bank. I thought of Pauline. I couldn't imagine her with two black eyes, with her jaw somehow twisted. I didn't understand. I called my father back.

"Where is she? What hospital?"

"Memorial. In Gardena."

She must have been so frightened, alone in a strange room after being pummeled like that.

"How did this happen?"

"We don't know," he said. "True, I'm going down there now. I'll let you know as soon as I know more. But don't let this screw you up. You're doing great."

I hung up and began hyperventilating, tears streaming down my face, but then I saw two teammates walking toward me, two big girls, Mia and Julie, heading out to practice, and I quickly wiped the tears away with the sleeve of my sweatshirt and turned toward the wall, picking up the receiver, as if I were still on the phone.

I went through our morning fitness like usual, and did turn-and-touch drills and one-pass-and-go as usual. I broke when the other girls broke, and ran at the front for each of our eight-hundreds, and finally, when we got back to scrimmages, I was, as usual, matched up against Alexis. At the start of the match, as Lorrie lazily rolled a ball to me and I flicked it back, Alexis ran up to press, and I turned, bumping into her, almost knocking her down.

"Watch it, you slut," Alexis said.

I ignored her and ran to a space on the right side, opening myself for a looping pass that I caught with my right foot. But then I made a sloppy second touch, too wide, and lost the ball to Michelle. I ran back down the pitch, passing Alexis, who had apparently decided that it was her day to wear me down.

"Fuckin' skank," she whispered.

I didn't engage her, keeping my head up, searching the field for gaps and space. I took a pass, one-touched it ahead to Lorrie, and turned and ran, Alexis intentionally lingering in my path so we made contact.

"Slut," she hissed.

I ran ahead, my head swiveled back to watch for Lorrie's cross, which came too high. I stopped, turned, jogged back.

"How's your retard sister?" Alexis asked.

That's when I stopped. I turned toward Alexis, put my head down, and was about to butt her in the nose with my forehead when instead I bent forward and bit her below the shoulder, my teeth sinking into her flesh. I don't know whether I tasted blood or imagined the taste, but I left a red mess on her white jersey between her breast and her right arm, an ovoid stain with unevenly spaced tooth marks. Alexis collapsed like a southern belle fainting at unwelcome news.

Everyone had seen it. The video cameras had caught it. I'd lost my composure in front of everyone. I swear, as I stood over Alexis, I could see her smiling up at me. I had broken her flesh, but she had broken me.

Fuck it.

Coach Tony ordered me off the pitch, back to the locker room. I was done for the day. I was to wait there until the rest of the team finished practice. Dr. Gifford found me where I was sitting, still in my practice kit, in front of my locker, and she told me Alexis was being taken to an emergency room for a tetanus shot and stitches.

There would be a team meeting that night to discuss my situation. I was to be showered and changed and waiting in the film room.

"Why?" Dr. Gifford asked me before setting off to join Alexis at the hospital.

I shrugged. I didn't know. Or I did, but I didn't. It was my sister. My heart had been broken. But I couldn't explain it, how it all fit together, how Alexis had said the wrong thing at the wrong time. Because the way my life worked, someone would always say the wrong thing at the wrong time.

I sat by myself in the film room for the three hours my teammates took to finish practice. I kept replaying the moment, marveling at the unlikeliness of it. How had I even found an angle to bite her chest? It was as if I'd opened my mouth and there was her clavicle, the fleshy patch below the shoulder. It was as if she'd turned toward me, and suddenly my mouth was filled with her sweat-wet jersey, salty against my tongue. It was as if my teeth had just snapped shut, like a reflex. My sister's jaw had been broken; mine was working all too well.

But biting Alexis hadn't felt like an aggressive act. That's what was so perplexing. It had felt like the only way I could pull Pauline through this hole in humanity, to the other side, where she would be a normal sister.

Alexis knew me too well. She knew the exact words to use and exactly when to use them. So she won.

Coach Tony came and collected me in the early evening, his expression blank, never making eye contact. He took me into the meeting room, where the chairs had been set up in a circular pattern, and I was to sit in a solitary chair in the middle. There were all the big girls—Mia, Michelle, Shannon, Briana, Brandi, Julie—showered, massaged, dressed in their travel wear, skirts and blouses; and there was Alexis, in an elaborate bandage and sling, sitting and looking downward. The Under-23s and Under-17s were also there, some of them sitting in the circle, others around the outside of it.

Coach Tony began, saying that the team had something to tell me and that they'd go around the room and each girl would tell me specifically how I had disappointed her. The theme of the complaints was familiar: I had betrayed the team. They loved me and hoped I would get the help I needed. But my presence here made them feel unsafe. Oh, they respected me. But I wasn't a good friend, a good teammate. Some of the big girls even complained that during Three Nations, they never saw me outside of practice. They said they saw Tricia, the alternate goalie, all the time, but they never saw me. Of course, Tricia's parents had rented a suite at the team hotel. I'd had to stay at the pension. I started to say that I'd been an alternate and tournament rules meant I couldn't stay at the same hotel—but Coach Tony told me I had to sit and listen. Be silent.

I couldn't defend myself, and the girls kept weighing in with how they couldn't trust me, how they were frightened of me, how I'd created an unsafe environment.

Every big-girl midfielder, it seemed, was particularly critical of my behavior. That made sense. I was a threat to them—but not because I was a physical danger.

Finally, Alexis spoke, looking downward, demure, wincing.

"True," she said. "We've been teammates for like forever, and we've not always been the best of friends, but I've always respected you and treated you with respect, and that's why this hurts so much. I know you've had a hard time, or haven't had the same opportunities some of us have had, but that doesn't mean you should take your jealousy out on me like this. I mean, my parents pitched in to pay for your travel like a hundred times in regionals, so, I mean, it's like, really hurtful that you would do this to me, when we've always been there for you. I'm, I'm like shattered and almost feel like giving up, like leaving rezzies—"

Murmurs of "No," "No way," "Not fair" went up around the circle.

"I'm just so hurt."

I stopped listening.

Dr. Gifford and Dr. Dorfman were standing behind the girls, and I avoided making eye contact with either of them.

I met with Coach Tony after the team meeting. I sat on a sofa perpendicular to an armchair, across from a coffee table on which he'd set a whiteboard showing a diagram of a play we called Mia 5 but that was just a variation on Barcelona 5. Basically, a midfielder kicks the ball out to a winger, and then the winger has to make a quick decision to push or to turn toward the middle. The key was for the winger to draw two defenders, freeing up the initial passer, usually Mia. It was a simple play, but there were a dozen variations. Like most soccer plays, it never unfolded on the pitch as it was drawn; defenders wouldn't take the bait, or our own formation would be too bunched, or the girl receiving the pass would drift offside. Soccer plays tended to be concepts that you kept in mind and tried to superimpose over the chaos on the pitch, but sometimes they resembled real live soccer as much as Monopoly resembled the real estate business. Coach Tony had always complained that he didn't feel he got much buy-in from me on his carefully diagrammed plays.

He was right, but that was because I could keep more permutations in my mind than just his plays. I saw the pitch better than any of his other girls. I could see where those dumb ball watchers were going before they did. But then why couldn't I see where Alexis was going when she began her line of attack?

I fell for it. I couldn't see shit.

"I have four girls coming in," Coach Tony said as he sat in the armchair, "and we need to make space. So I'm sending you home, True."

"Uh-huh."

"I don't see that I have a choice," Coach Tony said. "You're a terrific player, but the girls are really uncomfortable with you on the pitch right now. You heard them."

"So they decide who stays or goes?" I said.

He shook his head. "My call."

I nodded.

"And True. You'll never get a run if you can't control your temper," Coach Tony told me. "That was one of the cheapest shots I've ever seen. And in a scrimmage."

I nodded my head. "My sister—"

I began crying, gasping a little as tears welled and streamed. I wanted to explain what had happened to my sister, or what we thought had happened, but I couldn't. I felt ashamed, because I had let Pauline go. I should have been there with her, or she should have been here with me. I couldn't explain that to Coach Tony, and I wasn't sure any of it made sense, so I just dried my tears and asked, "What about the national team?"

He shook his head. "There's not a fit right now. We're loaded with midfielders."

Chapter 24

Statistically, a developmentally disabled teen is twice as likely to be physically abused as a developmentally typical teen, although accurate data is hard to come by because of underreporting in cases where the victim is nonverbal. She is more likely to be physically abused by a family member and three times as likely to be abused by a caregiver or stranger. Again, the vast majority of these cases go unreported or cannot be investigated because of the inherent unreliability of a developmentally atypical—often nonverbal—victim. In cases where the caregiver or a fellow client of an institution or assisted-living facility is the likely assailant, the victim's only recourse is to leave the facility. Statistically, a developmentally disabled female is three times more likely to be physically abused than a similarly disabled male. An assailant of a developmentally atypical female is one-fifth as likely to be prosecuted as an assailant of a developmentally typical female.

Pauline was in the hospital for five days, during which a surgeon attempted to reconstruct her jaw, and then wired it shut. Her eyes healed slowly, the sockets returning to their natural color in just forty-eight hours but the puffiness lingering for a week. The primary issue, Dr. Kim, the maxillofacial surgeon, informed us, would be her jawline, which might never again be as perfectly symmetrical as it had been. He would do his best, he promised, but one could never predict how fused bone would heal, especially in the face. Pauline could end up looking a little, um, different.

When my father was called in and Pauline was made to feel safe enough to describe what had happened, she eventually made clear that Rod, a boy prone to head butting who was strapped into a football helmet much of the day, had attempted to rape her in her room, while psych techs were present in the house. She had successfully resisted, and in his frustration, he had punched her, openhanded, palms against her face, scratched her arms in eight places, and head-butted her chin with his forehead. All of this was in her medical record.

The psych techs hadn't seen or heard a thing. They found her in the morning, crying and hiding under her bed.

My father didn't tell me any of this. I read it in badly cropped photocopied case files that were sent to the house.

The parents of the boy, Rod, were refusing to remove him from Found Horizons or to admit that Rod had in fact done anything wrong. The Regional Center representative, as well as Sylvester from Found Horizons, was urging my father to drop the matter. No one was allowed to interview Rod without an attorney present, and Rod's testimony was unreliable. As was Pauline's.

But there was no doubt that Pauline had been injured, more damaged now than the girl who'd been admitted to the facility. Even when she returned from the hospital, her jaw wired shut, her weight plummeting despite a half dozen Ensures a day, she shied away from all contact, even from me, and it took almost a week for her to relax and let me hug her. I didn't like to think about what had happened to her, what she had gone through, so instead I began to blame my father, insisting we'd known all along that that place was no good for her.

He said he'd done the best he could.

My father started listening to a series of therapeutic cassettes to help him sleep, a steady, droning, reassuring voice that urged him to relax each finger, to feel his hands grow heavy, to relax his hands, to feel each hand settle into the mattress, to let go. He began to listen to this cassette even when he was still awake, in his bedroom, looking through yachting magazines. He put it on as soon as he returned from Hops, as a steady accompaniment to his life with us. To feel each toe relaxing, then his foot, his leg. To imagine each leg drifting, floating . . .

The day after a Panorex X-ray confirmed that Pauline's mandible was healing, Dr. Kim removed the wiring from her teeth, and Pauline attempted to move her jaw. The surgeon claimed to be happy with the outcome as he gently turned her face in his hand, from left to right and back, and observed that there would be more settling of the bone and muscles now that she was healing. There would be more ice, and then more hot pads, alternating every fifteen minutes for the next few weeks. But considering the fracture, he felt she was healing nicely.

"D-d-do I look like me?" Pauline asked me.

I lied and told her yes.

But she looked a little different, just a touch, a slight underbite now coarsening her fine features. She was still very pretty, but she had been, of course, beautiful.

For her first meal of solid food, Pauline wanted some sweet-and-sour pork. I took her down to Hops. Fernando already knew that I hadn't made the team. He told me I could always have a job there, with him.

I ordered the sweet-and-sour pork and the fried rice to go and brought it out to the car, where Pauline waited. Back at our kitchen table I fed her, one spoonful at a time. I wanted to make her strong again.

Every Division I college rescinded its offer. UC Miramar, a Division II school, was the only college that said it would still offer me a full ride.

I watched the 1999 World Cup on television with a few other players from the UC Miramar squad. We were in the living room of an off-campus house shared by a few of our seniors.

Considering that this was the game that would establish the Women's World Cup as a must-watch sports spectacle for Americans, it was a surprisingly tepid affair. Julie, Mia, and Brandi played well, and Alexis played a brilliant game, controlling the midfield, but I believed the team lacked cohesion, lacked that one player who could make surprising runs or find open space. I could see the missing player, and the missing player was me.

I knew I was supposed to be rooting for the American women, for my former teammates, but secretly, I was elated when China's Fan Yunjie headed that ball that looked like it was going in, and I was deflated when Kristine cleared it off the line.

When Alexis scored the winning goal in the shoot-out, slipping one into the lower left past Gao Hong, I sat there while my UC Miramar teammates cheered. Alexis ripped off her jersey, and that photo of her in her sports bra ended up on the cover of *Sports Illustrated* and *Time*. She became the most famous female soccer player in America.

BOOK II

2004

Chapter 25

Here's what all those parents of all us girls who play organized soccer don't know. After the club and high school and college games are all done, we have nowhere to play. Boys have been playing pickup soccer their whole lives, four-on-fours in front yards, on paved streets, in parking lots with trash cans as goals, but girls don't play pickup, not often. When I was young, with the demands of playing every day for club or NSCAA or high school, I didn't notice. I always had a game. There were always girls to play with me. But now if I want a game, I have to go find it, which is why I am here on a Wednesday afternoon, putting the second of a brace—a ball I have to untangle from under my feet with a tasty little back foot tap—into a small goal while a big, dumb Argentine named Giacomo gasps and says, "What the fuck was that?"

"That was a girl scoring a beautiful goal on you, is what that was," says a suede-headed Asian named Tomo.

And I run back down to my side. The team I just scored against leaves the pitch, all salty, and another team comes on. Several times, as I'm taking the ball up, I receive a hard challenge, which is the ultimate sign of respect for me—that a man will try a tackle, even in a pickup game. He'll take me down, a hard foul, but I'll pop right back up, because it takes more than a hard foul to knock me out of the game. This is why I like playing with men: I can push them back. I can get leverage with an occasional elbow, and the boys are reluctant to complain that a girl is playing too rough. So foul me, hard, push me, knock me around, because then I can retaliate with good clean violence.

We win seven straight games, until half our squad is so exhausted that we give up a cheap nutmeg goal. Then we walk over to the fence where players waiting to come on the field mill about and kick around, and we sit down, happily spent, and I've earned every bit of acceptance from the men around me, and they've forgotten, I like to think, that I'm the girl.

Behind us, skirting the park, is a busy two-lane street. The rush-hour traffic passes in a static wash of sound that becomes noticeable only when a throaty Harley roars past or a truck engine chugs and rumbles. I pull off my shirt, leaving only my sports bra. Digging through my duffel, I take out a dry T-shirt and slip that on, then a hoodie. I remove my cleats, feel around my toes gingerly, checking for more damage, and then step into my slides. I stand up, brushing grass from my shorts.

"I'm out," I say quietly.

While I'm walking back toward my car, I pass Tomo, who's drinking water from a plastic jug. He looks up at me.

"You play good," he says.

I nod. I'm used to it. I'm waiting for the bullet: *for a girl*. But it doesn't come, and I'm grateful for that small gesture.

"You played in college?" he asks.

I nod.

"Where?"

"UC Miramar."

He nods. It's just a college to him. He doesn't see it as a billboard of my disappointments and failures. He doesn't understand that it's not the University of Denver, North Carolina, Santa Clara, UCLA—the powerhouses of women's soccer that feed players onto the national team. Two of my high school classmates ended up at UCLA, a third at Boston University, another at North Carolina, and one on the national team. Two if you count me. But did I really make it?

"You were the best?" Tomo asks. "In your college. The best player?"

Was I the best? I was the only player invited to the Olympic Development Program, the only player who'd been chosen for a national team residency. I was a first-team all-American sweeper my junior year on the team and would have played for the Division II championship if I hadn't collected a red card on my second yellow of the tournament, for elbowing Erika Alfredson in the back of the head and knocking her unconscious. The best? Yes, I was.

"You play hard," Tomo says. "Maybe too hard."

I force myself to smile. So often players have held their hands out, horizontal to the ground, making a slight downward gesture and saying, *"Tranquila, tranquila, señorita."* The language of pickup football, I have found, is Spanish. No matter where the player is from.

I shrug. I'd rather fight a man six inches taller than I am who outweighs me by sixty pounds than play soft. Hard is the only way I can play. Mia Hamm, during my residency, called me the bitch of the pitch, and I took it as a sign of respect.

Tomo stands up. He's shirtless, revealing a hairless chest, tattoos swirling up both his arms, and a pair of crossed samurai swords inked beneath his navel. He wears little white canvas shorts with pockets, and his legs are still padded and cleated.

"Hey, maybe I'll call you sometime," he says.

"Why?" I ask.

He laughs. "Why? So we can talk about soccer."

I nod and give him my phone number.

"I hope you don't drive like you play soccer," he says, "or I'd hate to see the condition of your vehicle."

Why does he like me? Does he like me? I told you, I'm invisible until the game begins, and then . . . I will haunt you.

Chapter 26

Tomo calls me the next day. I'm feeding Pauline chicken pot stickers and rice, and trying to convince her to eat some broccoli, which she resists. I've removed her helmet so she can eat, and her hair's surrounding us in a foul-smelling wave. I have to wash her hair; I have to cut her nails; I have to insert a tampon; I have to wipe her.

"D-d-d-d-d-d-d-d-d," she mumbles.

He's at work. Our father has unsuccessfully transitioned from feckless financial adviser to crappy real estate agent. The trunk of his GMC Jimmy is loaded with "Open House" signs, his face on business cards and in the local paper, usually next to a listing for one-bedroom condominiums on our town's main thoroughfare.

"Working," I tell Pauline.

She looks at me, smiles, rocks back and forth, enjoying the bite of chicken in her mouth. "T-t-t-t-t-t-t." She leans her head against my shoulder. Trudy.

I pat her smelly hair.

She stuffs her mouth as full as she can. She doesn't believe in delaying gratification. Whatever is good must be consumed now, before the plate disappears.

She's learned that from years of institutionalization, from hard time done in state facilities like Fairview Developmental Center down in

Costa Mesa and Maupin over in La Crescenta, unhappy stretches where we've tried to find a place for Pauline, with disastrous results.

She's home now, back in her old bedroom, and as long as I'm here to feed, clothe, and bathe her, my father and I can work in shifts to keep her alive. I take the mornings and early afternoon, Dad comes home from midafternoon to early evening, and then I return from pickup soccer and clean up whatever mess has been left.

Pauline's made some small strides. Her vocabulary, stutters and all, is up to a hundred and fifty words. She doesn't wet herself. She brings her dirty clothes to the hamper. She carries a dish to the sink. But our house is still a wreck: tables overturned, walls smeared with food, piles of garbage spilling over into piles of laundry near the washer and dryer. My father was never a tidy housekeeper in the best of times, but while I was living at home, he made an effort, picking up socks and underwear, giving the cereal-strewn linoleum a cursory once-over with the vacuum cleaner. But when I went away to college, when we attempted to find a place for Pauline, he let the house go. Ironically, this was when he started studying for his real estate license exam, when he was beginning the process of passing himself off as something of an expert on where and how to live.

We are held together by my will, my father's resignation, and Pauline's bottomless ability to absorb everything we have. A house is not a home, of course, without the sum of the suffering and fury being outweighed by love and hope. Love, it turns out, isn't always enough. A girl can love her dog, I'm sure, but should that dog become incontinent, occasionally take a bite out of her, and shit persistently on her bed, she may well overcome her love and get rid of the pooch. It takes hope for positive change to make the math of our house add up to a home.

So I feed Pauline and then run her a bath, dunking her into the warm tub, a luxury for her after the rushed showers of group homes and institutions. She lays her head against me and smiles, the bliss of hot water, bubbles, a soft washcloth, my hands wiping soapy water from her eyes. My sister, my lovely sister, is still beautiful after all she's been through, still eliciting catcalls from strangers when I take her to the supermarket, but she can barely string together a sentence.

"I l-l-l-l-l-l-l," she says.

"I love you too."

I tell Pauline that Dad's at work, but the truth is, I take the evening shift at home so he can retire to Hops, where the gang of middle-aged petty gamblers of roughly the same shape and size as the men in the gang from my high school years huddle around their card games, with Cutty Sark or Seagram's 7 in rocks glasses. The now potbellied Mexicans, Fernando and Carlos, sling food from an updated menu, tacos and tortas added to the typical mix of Chinese dishes. I hesitate even to ask my father to take an evening with Pauline so I can go out on a date with Tomo.

But Dad smiles and nods when I do, happy for me. "That's great, kid. Good for you."

"You promise?" I say.

"Sure!"

But on the evening in question, I have to hustle Pauline down to Hops. I leave her in the car while I head upstairs to roust my dad, who's buzzed from a few Cuttys but still fit enough, I determine, to prevent Pauline from drinking drain cleaner.

I tell Tomo I'll meet him at a bar in Santa Monica, a few miles south of Pacific Point. The place has sawdust on the floor and old brandy bottles shaped like cannons and galleons on a shelf above the active top-shelf bottles. The forced cheeriness, the wink-wink chalkboard specials for Sex on the Beach or Afternoon Delight make me anxious, as if I'm too somber for this bullshit chitchat of happy-hour drinkers. But then I look around at my fellow patrons and tell myself that we're all just trying to get by, so I take my place at the trough, order a gin and tonic, and then feel a tap on my shoulder. And there is Tomo.

He's handsome, actually, I realize, in street clothes—tall, with angular features, a narrow, stubbled face that could claim as its provenance any of a half dozen Asian countries, large brown eyes with epicanthic folds, thick, bushy eyebrows, a forehead that blends with his shorn head. Which leads me to my next thought: *What does he see in me?*

When I'm off the pitch, I reduce myself to my worst features: my crooked nose, my gnarled toes, my damaged sister. But I have to remember, Tomo met me on the pitch, saw me at my finest, so why shouldn't he be here with me now?

"You came," he said.

I shrugged. *Of course,* I think, *look at you!* "Yeah."

The awkward first few silent moments are finally broken when he signals for a drink.

He tells me his parents are Japanese, or Koreans who lived in Japan before immigrating to the United States. Which makes him sort of both, or neither. The Asian kids at Venice High School weren't so discerning; they banded together based on region rather than country. Through soccer Tomo became teammates and friends with Mexican and Salvadoran players, and his squad took Venice to a city semifinal.

I'm full of questions: Did he ever play Tri-County? Regionals? Select? Who was his coach, his technical adviser? I run down a list of male players from my era, and he recognizes a few of them.

"But whoa, whoa, I didn't play in college—I didn't even *go* to college, so . . ."

He has an older brother, a younger sister—she's playing at Culver City High School—and tells me he spends his days working for his older brother at a shop that customizes and fixes Porsches. But he drives a Mitsubishi Lancer Evolution.

He looks around, nodding. He has a stolidity that I find comforting. But then I realize he's waiting for me to fill in the silence with small talk. From me? Good luck.

We're at a conversational impasse, but instead of feeling uncomfortable, it's soothing, and after another drink, I find that my hard edges are melting away. He has an easy, friendly nod, a bob of the head like a beach ball floating in rippled water, that gives his conversation a pleasing rhythm. But beneath the winning features, under his calm, I can feel the hustle, the street. And as he talks, he hints at a past more violent than even my own—or, at least, more violent in the real world and not on the pitch. Through his soccer teammates, he got mixed up in some Venice youth-gang action, not a Ghost Town V13 set—or, well, yes, it actually was, a Li'l Jokers crew, but in a strictly auxiliary capacity. "No ricers," he says. He was inked but has since covered those letters and numbers with an elaborate yakuza-style tattoo. One I've seen, the crossed samurai swords below his navel.

"What? So you're like a gangster?"

He laughs. "Nah. I shouldn't have even told you so much. It's just . . . nerves."

"Jail?"

He shrugs. "Juvie. Once. Probation. Once."

"Why?"

"Just fighting."

"Fight on the field and all you get is a red card," I tell him. But as soon as I say it, I realize I'm wrong. I got so much worse.

It's hard trying to transfer a soccer relationship into a real relationship. And it's hard for me to have a relationship period.

Tomo asks me whether I smoke. I tell him I don't but I'll stand outside with him while he does.

He's long and thin, an overgrown boy, all of him—cheekbones, elbows, knees in his skinny jeans—protruding and jagged, a slender punk in a yellow cone of light cast by the gooseneck fixture above the bar's sign. He nods at me as he smokes. I find myself nodding back. I feel like we get each other.

A thick-chested middle-aged man with brown and gray hair extending like scouring pads from around a bald spot stumbles from the bar with a blond-haired woman with what appears to be a pair of black eyes.

I'm watching the woman, and so is Tomo.

She sees us staring and says "Botox" as an explanation.

"You don't need to tell 'em anything," the man says, waving a tattooed tan trunk of an arm. He's wearing an old Maui and Sons T-shirt, and beneath it I can see he's got some bulk, a thin layer of fat coating muscular slab. "Don't need to tell that gook nothin'," he mumbles, lighting a cigarette. He's slurring his words and has his vast back to us, but I can see there's an alert aspect to the way he's standing, a tension in the rigidity of his shoulders.

"The fuck you say?" Tomo says.

I'm about to take Tomo by the arm, but he's already put out his cigarette and shifted his weight forward.

"This ain't Moanalua Road, boy," the man says. "I saw plenty of your kind in the service. Took all your shit at Pearl. Don't need to take it here."

"What the fuck you talking about, old man?"

Now the ex-navy man turns around and sizes up Tomo.

"Just leave him alone, Ray," says the woman. "He's just some kid."

But Ray's face turns red, and he mumbles about getting "beefed" by a bunch of Hawaiians just off base at Pearl. And he's not gonna take any more gook shit now that he's mainland-side.

I'm tempted to play peacemaker, to step in and pull Tomo away, but I'm also completely fascinated. I want to see some action, to see the two men have it out. So I just stand there while Tomo makes a quick and sudden lunge, and lands a punch to the solar plexus that sends Ray to the ground, coughing, cigarette flying through the night like ember spark from a fire, and leaves his woman gasping in surprise. I look down at the crumpled couple, and then, excited by the violence, I whisper to Tomo, "Let's go somewhere and have sex."

He nods, opens and closes his fist a few times, and heads inside to clear the bar tab.

"Oh, Ray," the woman is saying, bruised eyes dripping with tears. "You're not eighteen and in Subic Bay, for god's sake."

Tomo drives me to his brother's garage, where a pair of Porsche 911s are parked in front of the lowered service-bay doors, and inside, another pair of Porsches are on lowered hydraulic lifts. The dried engine oil on the black floor reflects the white streetlight through the service-bay windows until Tomo hits the lights over the workbenches on the far wall of the garage. I make my way cautiously along the soft, slick cement floor, and then he turns and bends down and takes me in his arms. I shake my head, pull away, take his fist—the fist that punched the ex-sailor—and study it for bruises, for marks, for blemishes. A thick, gnarled hand, knuckles flattened; it's a tool, often used, used well.

There's an office to the side, and a waiting room with a brown leather sofa, soft, forgiving, where too many asses have probably waited out the completion of paperwork before gathering their 964s or 993s, but when he lays me down on it, it feels like a captured bit of cloud, and his weight atop me is a relief, a pressure that depressurizes me, and when my pants are off and his are at his ankles, when he pushes in, I am centered, calm, tranquil. *Tranquila.* Sex, for me, when it works, feels like soccer.

Chapter 27

I've never been datable. It's not my body; it's my personality. I've known that since high school, but it doesn't stop me from wanting a boyfriend, a relationship, regular sex, a non-soccer-related endorphin release. But I don't need it, I remind myself, as Tomo drives me back to my car after our night of fucking in his brother's repair garage. We are pathetic, the two of us, twenty-three-year-olds who have to shag on an office sofa because we both live at home with our parents. But then, I'm playing soccer in pickup games on high school fields when I should be playing for the national team. I'm used to doing things in places I'm not supposed to.

We're silent in the car, and while Tomo drives, I study his profile, the lean, hungry set of his expression, the squint as he scans the road, the deft clutchery with the stick. I want to see him again already, but I'm careful not to want him too badly, because when I want things too badly, I lose them, get carded, sent off. So I'm going to force myself to take what's there, to run into whatever open space I see, but nothing more. A lucky night, perhaps another; that's how I have to see him.

It would be improper, self-defeating, for me to ask for more. Statistically, relationships tend to be formed by similarly attractive partners, like my parents, and here it's obvious that we're asymmetrical. Tomo is better looking, and nines don't date fives.

The only thing that gives me a chance is that he noticed me first on the pitch, and there, even I would argue, I'm a ten. So when he drops me off, I tell him to call me.

He nods. For sure.

And whatever worked for me that evening must have worked for him, too, because we see each other twice more that week. I drive to the garage after putting Pauline into bed. I know it's irresponsible, leaving her alone at home, but okay, I'll be irresponsible for once. When Tomo texts me the next evening, I tell myself I can't leave my sister again. I can't. That would be forsaking her to satisfy myself, an abdication of my duties. But then I think of him pressing into me, his shape and size, and the feeling of escape, of freedom, and then I respond, and then I drive to him, leaving Pauline, taking that chance.

We fuck. Savage. I'm on top, and then he gasps, shocked, at what he sees when he looks down. Blood. Blood everywhere. As if he has actually ripped me open and I'm spilling my guts.

I'm embarrassed, apologetic. My period has come early, and we scramble off the sofa. We have to use up a blackened oil rag from the garage and the entire supply of paper towels from the dispenser in the bathroom to wipe off ourselves and the sofa, a grim chore that we undertake as a team, with quiet concentration, every corner and crevice of that leather sofa scrubbed clean.

And I'm home before my father returns from Hops. I'm in the bathroom, grabbing a tampon, when I hear him finally stumble in, the clank of keys on the entry table, footsteps past the kitchen to his bedroom. The television turns on. From my bedroom, I can hear a hyped-up *SportsCenter* voice tell us it is . . . going, going, gone.

Tomo calls to ask me if I'm going to the Argentine and African game at UCLA. He's off work today and looking for a kickaround. I say I'll be there, and he says he'll pick me up, make the long swing up from Venice to Pacific Point, and then we can drive to the pitch together.

I pause. The only time I rode with other players was when I was on a youth team, or back at UC Miramar, or, of course, on a plane with the national team. If I ride to the pickup game with Tomo, that means we're like a team, arriving together, gathering our kit, stretching, and I think that it's a bit . . . early for that.

I tell him I'll meet him there.

When I arrive, Tomo's already running with a strong six of African players and frat boys—pickup soccer in Los Angeles cuts across every demographic and racial boundary, gardeners playing with their employers, blond Swedes playing with dark, dark Senegalese. Girls playing with boys. I sit down, prepare my feet, my boots, and my kit, and stand near the northern goal, where teams marshal for the next spot on the field. There's already a team waiting, but when Giacomo, the Argentine I scored against the day I met Tomo, spots me, he tells another of the waiting players, "You're out. She's in."

The ultimate praise for any female soccer player: usurping a boy. I take my place on the sidelines, and when Tomo's side scores, we come onto the pitch, six of us going to our natural positions. I have to defer to another player who also wants to play center midfield, so I slide to the right. In small games, positions matter less than personalities and style. I'm a fast study, quick to understand how a player plays and to figure out how to maximize his talents, as limited as they may be. I'll pass you the ball once—in a good spot, twice—and if you can't do anything with it, or if you lose it, then you will never see the ball again, not from me. I'd rather take my chances solo than pass to a weaker player. It is, in other words, the opposite of high-level team soccer.

Tomo and I barely acknowledge each other during the game. We're matched up one-on-one a few times, and each time, I'm past him quickly, too quickly. At one point, when we're both standing, hands at our hips, watching a player run to retrieve a distant out-of-bounds ball, I tell him, "Don't fucking do that."

"What?"

"Let me beat you." I turn to him. "Okay?"

For a moment, he smiles, as if to deny tanking, but then he shrugs, nods. "Okay, deal. I'll never let you beat me again."

I scoff.

But the rest of the game, he's on me at my first touch like a husk, wrapping me, probing his long legs around me, using his size to move me off the ball, and the only way I can beat him is by pushing him off me, and when I do this, he looks around, as if to say, *See? She's fouling me.* I know that look. Girls have been shooting it to officials since I was nine.

But every good pass I make, every run around Tomo, is earned. Of that I am sure.

Finally, near the end of that first scoreless game, he slide tackles me, a rough hook that gets the ball but also takes out my legs. It's a hard foul, too hard for this game, for pickup soccer on a workday afternoon, but as I'm lying there, clutching my ankles, a crowd of boys around me asking if I'm okay, I'm thinking to myself, *Yes, yes, thank you, Tomo. Thank you for taking me down.*

"Why," Tomo asks, "do you never talk about your sister, your family?" He's told me about his family—I've already met his brother, who is so different from Tomo as to seem unrelated. He wears khakis and a button-up shirt to the garage and then changes into his mechanic's uniform. He's already married, with a baby, which means Tomo is an uncle. I will never have nieces.

"Why," he asks, "do you only like to talk about soccer?"

Because what else is there?

Chapter 28

Statistically, the father of a developmentally disabled child is more likely to consider suicide and to follow through on the act. He is more likely to develop chemical dependencies, more likely to die in a car accident or household fire. He is far less likely to describe his relationships with his non–developmentally disabled children, if he has any, as "stable" or "nurturing." He is more likely to have financial problems, more likely to have been arrested at some point in his life.

My father is hunched over the bar at Hops, downstairs instead of up in the card room, drinking a 7 and 7 with a twist, a baseball game on the television. He's rubbing the edge of a quarter against some Scratchers, blowing the waxy filings away, reading his losers.

"Your mother," he says. "She was a fine athlete. A great swimmer, a fast runner, great volleyball player. Born later, she would . . . could have done something with it. Like you did."

In photos, she's lithe but with great definition, every muscle where it's supposed to be without a single weight-training session or crunch. We have a home movie of her walking on her arms, on sand, going down the beach toward the breaking waves, somehow maintaining her balance. She was so strong, so powerful.

Even in Hops, surrounded by the sickly-sweet smell of alcohol and kitchen grease, I still like listening to my father tell stories about my mother's athleticism: when she dove—not jumped, but dove—off the ninety-foot board at Lake Elsinore, when she scaled a cliff face during a trip to Mexico. She'd never been a soccer player, he says, but she could have played any sport she wanted. Chosen any man she wanted.

"And she chose me," he says, smiling at his good fortune. "And you have her talents, her gifts."

Not all of them, I think. *Not the one that made her easy to love, not her beauty.* That went to Pauline. But I have her strength.

I'm waiting for my shift to start, and Pauline is out in the car. I do three nights a week at Hops, and as much as I like hearing about my mother, I need my father to get his ass up and back home. He's wearing a ridiculous Hawaiian shirt, a pair of denim shorts, socks, and sandals. You might buy a used catamaran from him, but not a house.

"Dad," I tell him, "you need to work on the wardrobe a little."

He nods. "Day off."

"A lot of days off."

He shrugs. He has no listings. I know the future weighs on him. What to do with Pauline. He's getting older. She's still a handful. But he can't face recommitting her to some state facility. So we're a tag team, each of us putting in shifts and each of us taking refuge where we can, me with soccer and Tomo, him with gambling, both of us in our own kind of denial.

"I'm thinking of sailing again," he says. "Maybe buying a little Hobie Mirage. They have these tri-hulls now. How does that sound?"

I shrug. Whatever.

I finally shuffle my father out to the car to drive Pauline home, and I head back into the restaurant, to families who'll come to nurse their children and cocktails simultaneously at the only place with a liquor license in a two-mile radius. I feel confined by the tables, the chairs, the uniform—black shirt, black trousers—my thigh and calf muscles bulging against the stove-pipe cut of my pants. I check the daily specials. The food—a mix of American Chinese and American Mexican—is salty fusion fare, having evolved under the guidance of Carlos and Fernando. Today we have the usual: crispy rock shrimp and spicy tuna tartare and jalapeño yellowtail and high-end pot stickers, which have become endemic to fusion-food joints. The kids will eat chicken nuggets and french fries.

We fill up quickly when the doors open at five in the evening, the stroller crowd occupying the darkened booths or the four-tops in the middle of the room, the singles crowding the bar, my dad's cronies melting away upstairs at the rattling pai gow table. Who owes whom is kept in a black ledger with red corners that Carlos meticulously updates, any money on the arm noted, the clock set to start running in twenty-four hours. How much does my father owe?

I don't ask. Not my problem. I made Carlos promise me that no matter what happens upstairs, I'll always get paid for my downstairs work. He's known me for over a decade, thrown a few hundred dollars into various plane tickets to various youth soccer programs. Discussed with me the European transfer windows, Andy Cole going to Manchester United, Vieri going to Juventus, and the possibility of Robinho going to his beloved Real Madrid. Invited me to watch the Champions League final in which Barcelona, whom he despises, defeated Arsenal. He's always a gentleman, and since he dyes his hair a deep blue-black and holds himself to a strict skin-care regime, he looks decades younger than he is.

I take up my station, input orders, and pony the drinks from the service well at the bar to thirsty parents, making sure sippy-cup apple juice is promptly delivered along with frosty martini glasses.

There's a Top 40 station playing tonight, a departure from the usual classic rock that the bartender, a white-bearded guy who rides a Harley, usually buttons in. No matter how peppy the jams, the joint is a narcotic fog of middle-aged desperation and alcoholism, grim parenting, and oversalted, oily food, the miasma of fryer oil and burnt fish hanging over the whole of the darkened room like a day's worth of bad memories.

As I'm standing at the bar station, waiting for the bartender to deliver a pair of pomegranate martinis, a man slides onto the stool beside me.

"Hey, True," he says.

I turn, and it's Brendan. I haven't seen him since high school, though, of course, I've *seen* him, in magazines, next to Alexis, the all-American couple, the camera finding him in the stands or posing shirtless with her in the Body Issue of *ESPN* magazine. I've heard he's still modeling, putting those angular and symmetrical features to work. But now, here he is, next to the service well at the bar.

"Brendan," I say. "Um, how's Alexis?"

He shrugs. "We broke up."

I've heard that before. I nod. "And you? How are you doing?"

"Good." He nods. "Really good. Surfing. Playing a lot of volleyball."

He'd played on the beach tour for a season, finishing out of the money in every tournament he and his doubles partner entered, but still, he was always described on television as Alexis's steady, "a model and professional beach volleyball player," though his income has always derived primarily from modeling for companies that sell volleyball shorts.

I wish he'd go away.

I gather an order onto a circular cork-lined tray and deliver it to a table; then I take the long way around the restaurant to another table, where more drinks are ordered.

During my periodic visits to the service well, Brendan tells me that he's living in a mobile home up in Malibu, in one of the trailer parks with ocean views, though he's renting on the cheap side of the lot without a peek of the sea.

While I'm waiting for a pair of mojitos—the bane of bartenders everywhere, all that mulling of mint leaves—I finally dare to look at him. He's still beautiful: the dismissive pout, the squinty gaze, the bushy eyebrows, and that chin, oh. And he knows it.

As I circle around the restaurant, he holds court. He's always seemed to know everybody everywhere he goes. He gets steadily more drunk, and we have less and less to say. He already knows my story. He saw it all from the other side. Finally, he asks if I'm still playing soccer.

I shrug. "A little."

By ten o'clock, when the dinner crowd has filed out and we're down to just the barflies, we have the space to talk more earnestly if we want, to bare our souls, but then what would I tell him? *You broke my heart?*

Instead, he turns that chin toward me and asks me to come up to Malibu with him, to his trailer by the sea.

I tell him I'm seeing somebody, but I know as soon as I say it that it doesn't matter.

The Pacific Coast Highway is a white ribbon of cadmium brightness unfurling between dark hills and black water. I lean my head against the window and feel the bumpy road on my forehead and think to myself, *This is wrong, wrong, wrong.*

Brendan is driving a new Jeep Cherokee, surfboard and wet suit in the back, and he smokes a cigarette that he holds out the window.

He's always looked so cruel, and when we pull into the trailer park and he parks on the crunchy pebble drive, I catch a glimpse of him that changes everything. That face that had once held so much sway over me, the fierce, angular perfection, now strikes me as awful, menacing. I don't need this. Not now. Not when I've got Tomo, a guy who's decent and likes me. But does Tomo actually like me? What's my worth outside of soccer? I've only ever been as good as my last run, my last touch, my last goal.

As Brendan leads me into his trailer, I can hear the ocean swells between the swishes of passing cars—a crash, a foam hiss. The air inside the trailer feels still after we come in from the coastal breeze. I feel my throat squeeze together, but I'm able to spit out one word: *"No."*

He turns. "What?"

"I can't do this now," I tell him, stopping cold.

He smirks, as if what I've just said is ridiculous, as if I'd asked to disembark from a flight in midair. He starts shaking his head, walking toward me.

No. No. No, his body language says. *You don't understand. I'm the one who decides when and where there will be copulation. Not you. You are the lucky chosen one.*

I start to back out of the trailer. It's dim, but I'm aware of jagged shapes, like arms, reaching up and all around me. I stick my hand out and hit a piece of driftwood, some sort of sculpture.

He takes my arm, pulls me toward him, pushes his face against mine, and when I don't reciprocate, I feel his muscles tense, hands digging into my arms. He laughs, as if to say, who am I to dismiss him, to reject him? That's not how this works. He's the entitled one.

I knee him in the balls and run from the trailer.

Chapter 29

Tomo's mother, Hiroko, is a Korean woman with large hips and thick calves but a pretty, unlined face. She greets me with a bow and invites me in, offering me a beer, which Tomo's father, YK, pours from a bottle. We drink our beer from small glasses, and nibble nuts and some kind of chewy dried meat from bowls on the coffee table.

The living room feels heavy and overstuffed, too small for the mahogany cabinetry, rear-projection TV, and sideboard bulging with family photos. YK and Hiroko sit in easy chairs, taciturn, nodding, asking about my family, my father, my sister. Tomo has already told them about my mother. I can feel them sizing me up, and I imagine they're wondering what their son sees in me. But they're unfailingly polite and gracious, and they listen as I tell them about my sister's disability, our family burden. They don't say anything, but I also imagine the calculations they're making about the kind of life their son would have with someone like me.

Or perhaps they're doing nothing more than trying to get through an awkward meeting with their son's girlfriend.

When Tomo invited me, he said it would be no big deal. But he also said that he didn't bring many girls home to meet his parents. "What makes me special?" I asked.

He shrugged.

But I know what makes us special. When we're together, we can spend long stretches gazing at each other, not speaking, not kissing, just in this silent, staring embrace. We can pass an hour at the Kubota German Auto Works just looking at each other. I've never experienced anything like that before, never lost myself in a partner. My college hookups had categorically been drunken bouts of fucking, usually rough, occasionally repeated, sometimes bruising, but without much pleasure and certainly without emotional engagement. And during the soccer season, I would shut that down so I could concentrate on footie. But here, with Tomo, with nothing else in my life to distract me, I've fallen into the kind of intense, adolescent longing that I haven't felt since, well, since Brendan. I never talk about it, because it feels both thrilling and revolting to need someone this much, to want him this badly, and to be able to stop time and just be.

Does Tomo feel it, too? Well, he asked me to his parents' house for dinner.

Tomo's little sister, Rie, runs downstairs. She's excited. Tomo's told her all about me, she says. She's a weedy girl, narrow calves, skinny thighs, no ass. But she's a soccer player, Tomo has told me. She asks if she can come and play pickup with us sometime, and I tell her it's fine with me.

She says that Tomo's told her that I knew the girls who won the World Cup in '99, that cadre of legendary players, and I tell her I did. I played with all of them.

"True got a four-year full ride," Tomo says. "Scholarship."

"For soccer?" Hiroko asks.

I nod.

The family is impressed. "Could you play pro?" Rie asks.

Tomo knows these are sensitive subjects for me, so he intercepts the question. "She's a great player. And hey, you remember Ricky Gutiérrez, kid who played with me at Venice?"

His parents nod, but I can tell this name doesn't mean much to them.

"Anyway, Ricky played in the MLS, two seasons, Seattle, got a sniff with the national team. Now he's an agent. He's sent a couple of players to play in Mexico, Turkey, has some players in the MLS. And he handles girls—"

I look at Tomo. I shake my head. This isn't the time or place to talk about something of this magnitude. "No—"

"Let's send him a tape," Tomo says. "Why not?"

He proposes this like it's a casual idea, a lark, like why not?

I grind my molars and stay silent. I can't believe he brought this up in front of his parents, and on our first meeting. He set me up. He knew I'd never listen otherwise.

But during dinner, a hot pot with pork, beef, cabbage, tofu, and mushrooms, all of it dunked in a garlicky sauce with grated radish, my anger burns away with the spices, and I mull it over a little. An agent? But I haven't even played on a club team since college.

The last time I joined a women's open-league team, it was too easy for me, and I lost interest after I realized I could beat every player out there without even passing the ball. So I quit and went back to playing pickup with the men. Since then, I've had some of my finest moments in soccer. But nobody who matters has been there to see any of them.

But Tomo should know I can't go backward. I can't undo my story and relive my glory days. I won't reopen that chapter of my life only to crush my dreams again and again. We drink our beer and eat the shabu-shabu in silence. Finally, I give him a look.

He smiles at me, nodding. "You can do anything, you know. *We* can do anything."

Tomo's eyes are sincere, and even though I know he appreciates my talent and believes in me, I also know he's manipulated the situation. He brought up Ricky in front of his parents because he knew I wouldn't storm out of their home in a rage. I would just have to sit there for an hour or two, with that thought out there, that proposition that I should try again. To reject that would be a quitter's move, and I'm not a quitter, or at least not when it comes to soccer. Part of me trusts Tomo completely, but part of me knows he's cunning, calculated on the field, artful. I also get the sense that he's not being honest with me.

The following weeks after the family dinner, Tomo disappears. He doesn't pick up his phone or answer messages. At first I imagine he's seeing another woman. But then he's back and as committed as ever. And then he's gone again. He won't explain to me where he's been or what he's been doing, and I become jealous, accusing him of hiding something. He admits that he has to go on errands—deliveries, so to speak.

"Delivering what?" I ask.

He shrugs. "Cars."

"You mean you're selling cars."

"Sort of," he says. I don't ask any more that night. But the next time we're at his brother's shop, I point to a metallic-blue 964 and tell him it's a cool-looking car. He nods. "It's a damn shame we're going to chop it up."

He asks me not to judge him, then explains that in addition to running a legitimate repair shop, he and his brother are operating a chop shop, busting up old air-cooled Porsches and even newer liquid-cooled models, which are frequently worth more divided into parts than they are as fully operable automobiles. The older-model Porsches in particular, the 964s and 993s, even original 911s, with their simple door-locking mechanisms and basic ignition systems, are easy cars to steal and frequently turn up on lists of most-stolen vehicles for a reason. Which means those cars sitting out there in dentists' driveways turn out to be nothing more than repositories of carburetors, crankshafts, valves, and manifolds, all the parts that Japanese lovers of old Porsches need to keep their vehicles running. The Porsche enthusiast in Tokyo, Japan, has two choices: buying ridiculously overpriced and tariffed parts from Porsche Japan or ordering them from Tomo and his brother. Both options are expensive, but Kubota German Auto Works is cheaper and, in many cases, faster. They rent half containers that depart Long Beach every few weeks. Occasionally, they send over entire cars, the chassis and engine-block numbers matching, the rest of the parts pulled from other cars. It's a lucrative business, he explains, and one made possible only by his family connections in Yokohama, where his Korean relatives work the docks and also middle the parts. His brother set up the racket, but Tomo is the key supplier.

He swears to me that he himself doesn't steal any cars.

But even as he's telling me this, I suspect it's sort of like me telling a coach that I don't intentionally foul anyone on the pitch. He's telling me what I want to hear. But he's a thief, my Tomo, a criminal. And as I ride around Venice with him one night, stopping into a few bars down near Washington Boulevard where a broad range of people, from younger Latinos to older, stubbled surfers, greet him with a bro shake and a half hug, I realize he's more connected to his little Westside gangster set than he's let on.

One day, when I go down to meet him at the Brig, he comes into the bar, and his eye is swelling and he's bleeding from his mouth. Before he even comes over to say hello, he goes to the bar and asks for ice, and the bartender looks him over and seems to be thinking of denying him service but then hands him a water glass filled with ice. Tomo sits down, but I'm so turned on that I take him by the hand and lead him out to his car, where I climb into the back, pull my sweats down, and pull him on top of me so that he fucks me while I rub my fingers over the hard, swollen flesh below his eye.

He's been in a fight, but he won't tell me with whom or why. He tells me only that I should have seen the other guy, how bruised and battered he was.

But it's when he meets Pauline that my heart melts. He sits down in the den, studies her for a while, nods, stands up, and walks over to my sister. She's assorting makeup pencils into piles according to length.

"Hey," he says, popping down onto the balls of his feet.

"T-t-t-t-t," she says. "Tomo."

He holds his hand up, not out to shake hands, but up, his palm outward. And for some reason Pauline holds her hand out, and they join them together, palm to palm. I've never seen her do that before.

She returns to her assorting.

Now whenever he comes over, he brings some *onigiri*, some orange chicken or sweet-and-sour pork, or some chicken teriyaki his mother has made, all packed into these little plastic compartmentalized containers with rice in one square, protein in another, and some pickled veggies, which Pauline won't touch, in another.

He brings her little presents: makeup, lip balm, eyeliner. She likes him.

Tomo's never been medicated, he tells me. He's smoked weed, done a little coke, taken some pills once in a while, but nothing on the regular. His drug of choice, it seems, is soccer, like mine. He's a clean criminal, and I have to admire his hustle in building this little enterprise.

When he moves out of his parents' house into a one-bedroom apartment on Pico, not far from Santa Monica College, I realize that Tomo is like a more successful version of my father, who spent his life looking for some angle or hustle but ended up saddled by his daughter, unable to ever really feel unfettered and free.

When Tomo and I are riding around in his Evolution or one of the Porsches with clean tags, on our way to a late-night ramen bowl, I feel like I'm catching a glimpse of this alternate future. Like maybe I can leave Pauline and my father behind, like I can join this other family, this criminal clan, and live on salty ramen and stolen cars and cum for the rest of my life. I could just ride away from Pauline and my dad. Could live with Tomo, play pickup soccer, smash anything or anyone that gets in our way, dribble right past them, go toward open space.

But then I have to check myself: I'm a twenty-three-year-old girl whose greatest talent is playing pickup soccer with a bunch of guys who themselves never made a dollar, euro, peso, ruble, or cruzeiro from the game. I'm a waitress still thirty credits shy of a BA, whose boyfriend is a car thief.

Chapter 30

Nobody paid any attention to women's soccer before Mia, Alexis, and those other girls won the World Cup in '99, but Tomo swears that Ricky, man, Ricky has heard of me. And he's interested. He says that the WUSA, the Women's United Soccer Association, which just recently folded, is looking to restart and there will be another draft soon. That Mia Hamm, Brandi Chastain, and all those other girls from the '99ers will also be in this new league. I don't tell Tomo that this isn't exactly an advantage for me.

"Just meet him," Tomo says. "Just hear him out."

"Why?"

"For me," Tomo says. "Prove to me that you were one of the best."

"You're challenging me?" I say.

He nods. "You know I am."

We meet with Ricky at a Starbucks in Venice, and he drives up in an M3, gives Tomo a big hug, and then shakes my hand and says that he's honored to meet me, that he's heard of me.

It's bullshit, but he's seen my Under-17 footage, some college highlights, my best goals in the Division II playoffs, even my national team appearance. I don't like to watch those videos anymore, though my father occasionally does. For me it feels worse than a broken rib to know that everyone else in the world has already forgotten about that girl on the tape. Though, in reality, I know that nobody could have actually forgotten me, because no one had ever heard of me, other than a few perverts and geeks who closely followed women's soccer. But the footage is beautiful: a girl with her head on a swivel, turning, passing, making quick runs, giving and going, everything at pace, every movement with a purpose, the lovely one-touch ball over and past Julie Monet in a scrimmage, the long, curving balls I ran under in the Under-17s against China, the broken nose against Mexico, being carried off, the long pass from Brandi that I caught on my toe on the right side of the box and then buried in a full scrimmage, that tasty second goal against Japan in Three Nations. Even against the best in the country, in the world, I'm a lovely player, or at least this video would convince anyone that I am. Many of the girls I'm playing against in this footage went on to play for their national teams, the Costa Ricans, Norwegians, Chinese—and here, look at all the instances when I'm their better.

Ricky was impressed enough to come and meet with me. I met with agents before, when the WUSA started up after the '99 World Cup, when I was drafted 103rd by the San Diego Orcas. Ricky's asked around. He's already heard about the fight I started the second day of Orca camp in Carlsbad, when I split Shannon MacMillan's lip and was asked to leave the team after that.

"Are you playing club soccer?" he asks.

We're drinking coffee at a little circular table in a courtyard next to a parking lot. I shake my head. "Just pickup."

"How's your fitness?" he asks. I shrug.

Tomo leans forward. "Dude, she outruns the boys at every game she plays."

Ricky says he'd like to see me play, maybe come and film me doing some drills with a proper team. He says he knows the Argentine game up at Will Rogers and he'll come for a kickaround.

I'm reluctant to talk myself up. I haven't played a meaningful game since the Division II playoffs my senior year of college, before I dropped out. But I feel like I need to come off as confident. After all, Ricky holds the key to my playing real soccer again, or maybe even to my getting paid for soccer.

But before I can say anything, Tomo says, "Dude, you'll forget she's a girl." Which is the greatest compliment anyone could give me.

—

When I tell my father about Ricky and show him Ricky's card from a sports agency that I'd previously never heard of, he nods, obviously wary. My soccer dreams were our family's dreams for so long, and when the hydrogen escaped from that zeppelin, it was a collective crash. We ignored it while I was in college—a college scholarship is still a great accomplishment—but when I failed to graduate, fell so many credits shy that after I'd used up my eligibility, they said I'd have to pay my own room and board to make up those remaining credits, we couldn't pretend anymore. At first I'd told myself I would make up those credits at Santa Monica College or UCLA summer school or somewhere else, but thirty credits, an entire academic year, was such a monolithic total that it seemed pointless to even start. So at the end of it, after the fifteen years of club soccer, the years of camps and regional teams, after all that, I was left without a degree and living at home.

Which is what we need anyway, I tell my father. Who else can take care of Pauline?

Ricky's card sits on the table between us, and I can read the lines on my father's face: he's reluctant to start redreaming soccer dreams. And really, what are the odds of another women's professional league ever starting? The last one, built on the heat of the '99 World Cup, collapsed after just a couple of seasons, so who could guarantee that a new league would do any better? But I still dream about soccer. So meeting with Ricky, talking to him about my game, and getting ready to play a meaningful game, even if it's just a pickup game, has me agitated all week. I even drive over to Latigo Canyon and run a few hummingbirds. I go down to my old high school pitch and run eight-hundreds. My wind isn't what it was, but I still feel fit, still feel strong.

And come Sunday, the Will Rogers game—a pickup match of Argentines and Italians, skilled players, tall, long haired, talented—I'm there early, stretched, warmed up. Ricky and Tomo arrive, and sides are chosen and divided according to whatever arbitrary process the Argentines and Italians decide among themselves. The game begins, and I am totally and completely in my world.

This is pickup, not league, so the spacing of the game is ragged, the players tending to bunch more around the ball, the defense less coordinated, but even in this pokey little game, I take up an offensive midfield position and begin directing players, waving an arm and pointing like a traffic cop. Ricky plays for the Argentines as well, same team as me. Tomo, as usual, is a striker for the other side.

There's a stocky Argentine on our side, surprisingly quick for his build, who typically waits for the ball on the other side's defense; he knows me, so whenever I catch a ball around midfield and turn, he takes off and finds an angle toward the goal. There's no official here, no offside flag, so I can take my time to pick out a moment when he's clear of the defense. By then, if defenders are closing in on me, I may have to quicken my pace, take the ball into the narrow gap between two defenders. But once I'm clear even a foot, I can turn, fire quickly, a ball off the outside of my right foot or a quick pop from the inside of my left. Give me eighteen inches, and I can find the trajectory to drop the ball on the head of a running striker.

It's a choppy game, frequently paused for theatrical gesticulations and operatic arguing among the Argentines and Italians, who on the pitch, at least, live up to every cultural stereotype. But after twenty minutes I prove to Ricky that I am what I say I am. He begins to drift forward, taking up a right-wing position, and I know he wants me to find him with a few wide passes, to see what it feels like to be on the end of my balls. Once I measure his pace, I pour a half dozen sweet gumdrops on him, some of which are a little too wide or deep, but which are also a message: I expect a faster player out there, better legs, more pace. He gets the idea.

After the match, as we're drinking water from plastic bottles, and the Argentines and Italians are continuing whatever arguments they've been having, Ricky says he wants to see me scrimmage with women players, in a proper game situation with an offside rule. I'm not real keen on playing with women, I want to say, but I stop myself. In college, when I wasn't playing varsity soccer, I played as the first substitute on a men's club team—I wasn't allowed on the official roster because of a league rule forbidding females—and since then, I've avoided female leagues; they just don't give me a match.

But if that's what Ricky wants to see, then I'll oblige.

He gives me a bro handshake, a bump, and says, "The girl can really play."

The Argentines and Italians, who apparently have been half listening, take a break from their bickering to chime in. *"¡Estúpido!"* one says. "Of course she can play!"

Tomo and I drive down to his apartment, where he lets me take the first shower. I rinse my hair, condition it, and watch the water run over my bloody and mangled toes.

Tomo is so delicate with my feet: he takes them, holds them in his hands, studies the arches, the mounds, the heel, the phalanges, the ankle, dares to lay a finger on the middle toe where the keratin is stripped and won't grow back, and on the always-broken little toe on the left foot. "I love your feet," he says.

"Why?" I ask.

"They're the only part of you that is weak."

I shake my head. "Not weak. Just a little, um, worn."

A soccer player will never admit to having foot problems. It's like a gunfighter admitting he has a slow trigger finger.

Chapter 31

Ricky meets Tomo and me at Kubota German Auto Works the Tuesday after the pickup game. He's all smiles.

"So you're the real thing!" he says.

"You couldn't figure that out for yourself?" I say.

"But people have heard of you. You're famous!"

"Infamous," I say.

He's asked around, spoken to some college coaches, some women's-soccer scouts. A few had been wondering what happened to me. They remembered me from rezzies, but then, in all the buzz and heat of the 1999 World Cup, the might-have-been stories tended to fall by the wayside. I was just another girl who hadn't panned out. Who knew why? Injuries? A pregnancy? A marriage? There were so many ways a girl could fall short, never mind just never living up to whatever potential she may have once shown.

"But coaches in, like, Japan, Denmark, Germany, they remember you," he says. "From Under-17s, from Three Nations. They always wondered why you weren't on the national team."

I shrug. "What's your take?"

"Finder's fee from the club, if you stick for a season," he says. "Half your signing bonus, if you have one. Five percent of your salary, seven if you're playing overseas. We can probably get some performance clauses worked into your contract. But I'm not getting rich here. Neither are you."

"Can I play in the US? What about that new women's league?" I ask.

He says he's not sure that will even happen.

But he calls me four days later with news. The WUSA is indeed relaunching with new sponsorship money from Nike and Powerade, a TV deal with Fox, and investment from Cox and Charter Communications. And the big news: the Los Angeles Fire is offering me a tryout. I imagine a thousand girls on a crowded pitch, a bunch of has-beens and never-wases, and me. But then Ricky promises, "It's a small squad practice, not some cattle call. You'll get a good look."

When I practice with the other top Los Angeles Fire prospects, I immediately appreciate that these are decent female players, but I still have to adjust my game a little; they're a half step slower than the boys on the pickup fields. The coach is a German woman, Ulrike, a veteran of their national team, and she has long, curly gray hair and wears these shimmery metallic-colored sweats and chews gum as she puts us through fitness drills. She has us doing the kinds of drills that I did as a fifteen-year-old, including a multiball drill that starts with receiving a through ball in, spinning, passing out, following the pass out, and then shouting for another ball.

She urges us to play the ball to the front foot—sharp, short passes. Then we are to spin and open for the return pass. I start dribbling, looking up for a player to pass to. The drill is as much about communication as passing, or it should be. The idea being that if we're not constantly talking to each other on the pitch, we'll keep the ball too long. And it's true. Communication is always crucial in soccer, especially in tight spaces, where you're more likely to have your head down. I make a strong showing, and these girls—several decent players among them, some top college players, as well as a few women in their twenties and even thirties who may have once been good players but are just a beat slow—run these drills efficiently enough. Soon, though, I find myself slowing and gradually losing interest. I'd forgotten the dull moments of institutional soccer.

When we finally get to scrimmaging, I quickly accelerate to full speed. These girls aren't quite good enough to get me the ball where I want it, so I slide forward to play striker, telling another player to move to my right. She looks at me with pursed lips, about to say something, but instead slides over. I take a ball near the top of the box, easily beat the thirtysomething marking me, and then bury the ball.

But I've stopped communicating. The coach, her wavy gray hair now tucked into a Nike cap, pulls me aside and asks me what's wrong. She heard from Ricky that I was a good player, and she can see that's true, but it doesn't seem like I'm having fun out there, getting the other girls involved, or playing with much enthusiasm.

I don't know what to tell her. That I'm the best player out here and this game is a little soft for my liking? I nod and tell her I'll talk to the other girls.

I retreat back to midfield and start collecting balls and distributing them around the pitch, shouting warnings at girls—look up, look up, *mira*, *mira*, go, go, turn, turn, *cambio*, *cambio*, on your back, on your back, *atrás*, *atrás*—since I don't remember any names.

Afterward, I can see the other girls are sort of trying to figure out who or what I am. Where I come from. And then one of them comes over and asks where I went to college. I tell her, and that doesn't really make sense to her, because she played for UCLA and I'm clearly a next-level player compared to her.

"You're a lovely player," she says.

I nod.

"Trudy," the coach says. "Good stuff. Good stuff. But a little more patience with some of the girls. We're team-first around here. And the attitude, it's—it's a little angry?"

"I play angry," I say.

"But we don't," she says.

Anyway, two days later, in a full-squad practice scrimmage, I put in a hat trick against the San Jose Shock.

I text Ricky after: how wuz THAT for game sitch?

The offer is faxed to Ricky's office on a Monday. The Los Angeles Fire will pay me $800 a game for a ten-game contract. The WUSA season is twenty-six games long, but Coach Ulrike is willing to take me only on a ten-game trial basis.

I tell Ricky I will so fucking take it.

So this is it then, I think as I drive home from a celebratory drink with Ricky and Tomo. I'm going to play with the best, or what passes for the best: the girls from the 1999 US team, the Chinese, Japanese, and Norwegian national team girls; the finest female players in the world have come to join the new WUSA. Ten games—six in Los Angeles, another four on the road—to prove that I belong in this league. I have no doubt that if I get on the pitch, I'll keep my spot. The question is whether Coach Ulrike will give me enough time to earn that spot.

The relaunch of the league is in the newspapers, the stories still skeptical about whether a women's league can succeed in America, considering one just folded last year. Fans just didn't watch in sufficient numbers to prop up the somewhat underfunded owners the last go-round. But this league is keeping costs in line, and even the assigned national and international players aren't getting the high six-figure deals they were coming off the '99 World Cup. Not that those girls earned their salaries: Alexis and the other girls had finished a disappointing third in the 2003 World Cup, losing to Birgit Prinz and the Germans in the semifinals. But even without a promise of big money, the '99 team was lucky to have a pro league to come back to instead of having to play overseas in the women's leagues in Norway, Germany, or Japan.

I feel a quickening in my heart that I haven't felt since I was invited to rezzies. After all the years away from organized soccer, all the pickup games, all the bald soccer pitches on smoggy days where the dirt swirls in the hot air and stings your eyes, the Mexican gardeners playing in their jeans and work boots, the trash cans for goals, the hundreds, maybe thousands, of boys I've schooled with a clever touch, I am finally going to get a chance to prove myself where it counts. Tomo has told me that I'm a diamond that's been hiding in plain sight, the best women's player in the country, and I'm kicking around the pickup games of Los Angeles. It's a great story, and now that it's finally happening, I've started to believe it.

"P-p-p-play p-p-pro?" Pauline says to me as I'm sliding off my socks after a game.

I nod my head.

She smiles. I've been playing soccer as long as she's been alive. She's been watching me her whole life.

"K-k-k-kick some g-g-g-goals."

The day after my offer, the *Los Angeles Times* runs a story announcing the league's player assignments. Most of the girls are joining up with teams in cities where they have some sort of local connection. I read that Alexis will be joining the Los Angeles Fire; I'm not surprised. I'd heard she was back in town, living with her new girlfriend, a former Olympic high jumper.

The next morning I hear from Ricky that the Fire has rescinded its offer to me.

Chapter 32

After getting so close with the new women's league, with the Los Angeles Fire, and then getting my offer withdrawn—again—I decide to abandon the dream of playing. Where would I play?

Norway? How could my father handle Pauline? She'd endured group homes and assisted-living facilities and state hospitals. Even after what she went through at Found Horizons, I still chose to go off to college instead of staying home with her. And while I was at UC Miramar, I imagined her as my very own real-life Dorian Gray portrait, her face fractured, her jawline never quite regaining its former sleek shape, as she wandered the hell of institutionalized care, narcotized on Zyprexa, Haldol, lorazepam, and Zoloft, the cocktail leaving her catatonic, prone to seizures, sleepy and then sleepless, a zombie whom I visited during my breaks, a lumpy—though still pretty—epigone of my sister. The visits left me shattered, and when I returned to my dorm at UC Miramar, I was unable to focus on my classes—or that was the excuse I used. I turned into little more than a sullen drinking partner.

My own medication was in flux, the Serzone replaced by Wellbutrin, but I went through stretches on and then off, always using my soccer game as an excuse. I said I felt sluggish on the pills, my game a millisecond off, so I discarded them, and in the off-season, I lost myself in the kind of binge drinking and hookup fucking that my classmates advocated. During the soccer season, I still wouldn't drink. I always took soccer fitness seriously.

In the summer I was no longer invited to rezzies; in the spring there was no longer an Under-23 slate.

My temper still occasionally got the best of me. I was sent off the pitch in seven matches during my collegiate career; I considered it a great achievement that I didn't bite anyone.

And when soccer season ended my senior year, my collegiate eligibility used up by December, I simply packed and left campus, driving up to where Pauline was staying at the Fairview Developmental Center in Costa Mesa. I did what I always did and drove her home against medical advice. My father had her legal conservatorship; I wasn't supposed to remove her, but I didn't give a fuck. And then we pulled up to our driveway, a pair of sisters, lots of bad news for my dad.

But as long as I was home, we could manage Pauline. A full-time job divided in two, caring for a twenty-one-year-old developmentally disabled girl. She could dress herself now, could shower, could even apply some very clownish makeup. Over the years, she'd been growing as well, albeit slowly, but who was I to judge, college dropout that I was.

My father urged me to get my degree. I was an English major, he reasoned, surely I could bullshit my way to another thirty credits at some extension program, get my degree, and become a high school teacher. But college without soccer made no sense to me, so I never went back. Instead, I jumped into the local pickup games and took a few nights at Hops, the hometown girl who once showed so much promise, carrying drinks on a round tray, dressed in a black shirt and tight black slacks.

I saw Alexis interviewed on ESPN, the prettiest of a generation of girls who'd become American heroes in 1999. At first the bartender, Terry, would turn up the volume when she appeared, having clocked that she was a local product, but when it became clear that it annoyed me, he kept the volume down. I watched her move her perfect lips, her fish-shaped eyes, her long, sharply bridged nose. She was still a beauty and still scoring goals for the national team and the Fire.

Did she ever think of me? Probably only when she felt the scar—there had to be a scar—where I took a chunk out of her.

"This isn't a life," Tomo tells me, "for me or for you." He's a car thief. I'm a waitress. We're like a couple in a film noir. There are no heroes.

We have soccer, I tell him. Great games. The Pauley Pavilion field. Will Rogers. University High School. Fairfax. The Persian game. The Argentine and Italian game. The Mexican game.

"That's fine for me," he says. "But you need a better game."

I'm stuck. My sister. My father. Pauline's doing so much better, I insist, since we pulled out of that last place, since I'm now around all the time. We've cut her meds. She's trying new foods. She can walk from our house to the village by herself, buy a frozen yogurt, and walk back home. I feel like shouting at Tomo, at the world, *Do you know how amazing that is?*

My father and I are terrified whenever she leaves home alone, but this is her, and our, greatest accomplishment. She's like a regular person, almost, when she makes that little walk.

It's a half mile to the village, and I watch her make her way down our driveway, take a right onto Papua Street, and then walk down Rushmore to the village, our hateful little town just a little less hateful, I think, if my sister can walk by herself those thousand or so steps, dressed in black jeans and a black T-shirt, her huge black eyes unblinking, her thick black hair brushed and tied back into a loose ponytail. The only thing that betrays her is her walk; it's still a little bouncy, on her toes, her gait too unnaturally up and down, her sneakers unevenly worn because her toes get so much more scuff than her heels. But there she goes, for all intents and purposes—if you squint, or look away quickly—a normal girl. I saved her from a state hospital, I tell myself. I gave her this life.

We can leave her alone for stretches. She won't drink the drain cleaner. Won't eat sand. Won't try to brush her teeth with an eyeliner pencil.

Not that Pauline's become a perfect little angel. Her advances are deceptive, and every time I think there's been bankable progress, she regresses. I return home from a shift at Hops, looking forward to meeting Tomo at his apartment, and I find that she's shit in her pants and fallen asleep on the sofa, leaving a fecal stain on our already-ratty three-seater. A small protest, perhaps, lodged against our increasingly erratic attention. Like a dog who's been left home alone too long, she protests with bowel movements.

Or it was just an honest mistake.

"See?" I assure my father. "She's getting better."

He nods and shrugs. He's watched her gain vocabulary, finer motor skills, greater self-restraint, only to slide back again. That's what's always been so frustrating about Pauline: how she so seldom holds on to her gains.

"But this feels different," I insist. "She's becoming more independent."

"Independent?" he says as he's wiping the shit stain from the couch.

I wish my father had a girlfriend, a friend besides the card players at Hops. I feel like I remember a more winning version of my father, who I knew for only a year or two, before the death of our mother, before Pauline, before what came after. I always had my refuge, my soccer, but what did he have? The demands of a family. I recall a few evenings in middle school when I would take care of Pauline so he could take out a local divorcée, but nothing ever came of these evenings, no lasting relationship, and now, as he slides deeper into middle age, I wonder if he's resigned to his solitude.

I tried to make him proud with my soccer, but my successes seemed to bore him at some point, so that by the time I failed to make the national team, he took it as a mild disappointment rather than the life-crushing event it turned out to be. It was only later, after I came home and started caring for Pauline, that I realized we'd never had one of those father-to-daughter conversations about how they were all bastards and I was his sweetheart. He never gave me a hug and said it was all right. He let me wallow in my own failure until even I grew sick of it. By the next season, I was back to playing my game, only now fielding offers from Division II schools willing to take a risk on a troubled player with violence issues.

It would have been easier to understand if he'd had a drug problem or a drinking problem, but instead, he had a disappointment problem.

I would move in with Tomo if it weren't for Pauline. We're spending more time together. He comes over sometimes and hangs out with the two of us, walks with us down to the village, sits with us at Hops, where Pauline eats her sweet-and-sour pork.

"B-b-b-boyfriend," Pauline says, smiling at Tomo.

I shrug. He nods.

We go out to the garage to look for more old videocassettes from my college and national team days. Tomo says he wants to see them, to transfer them to DVD. We go through the boxes of trophies, so many trophies, dozens of plaques—*City League First Team, NSCAA Regional Player of the Year, Parade Second Team All-American, Security Pacific Female Athlete of the Year*—and pull out a couple of tapes. I find the fragments of my father's unfinished novel shoved into a box up high on a shelf. And while Tomo sorts through the relics of my youth, amazed at the sheer volume of hardware I've won over the years, I read through the stack of pages.

At some point over the last five or so years since I first read these pages, my dad has added a few new chapters. The character of Bullet's baby sister has been changed. She's now a baby boy named Carson, and he's blind and deaf. And their mother has died—in a boating accident. The father doesn't know what to do with Carson, and he writes about him with almost diary-like repetition, the beads of worry and despair running through his mind. It doesn't seem like a novel anymore. It's just life.

Chapter 33

Tomo has started watching the DVDs of my old playing days over and over while he smokes a blunt. Suddenly, he's full of wisdom and advice about how I've let others define me, how I've let the national team girls—Alexis, Brandi, all of them—dictate how I've lived my life.

"Who cares what those girls think?" he asks.

I've just come out of the shower at his house, washing off from the Persian game at University High. A lazy, sluggish game undermined by the poor conditioning of the players—the best players hadn't showed up—leaving me unsatisfied and anxious. Tomo holds the blunt out to me, and I wave it off.

He turns off my DVD and switches the input so that he can play *Grand Theft Auto: San Andreas*. His least appealing trait, I suppose, is his very typical for his gender and demo habit of smoking weed and playing video games. He could lose more hours in this elaborate version of self-stimming than even Pauline could by rocking back and forth or assorting her makeup.

When I tell him he should be out doing something real, playing soccer or stealing an actual car instead of stealing cars in video games, he scoffs but continues playing. I know from watching him that locating and then swiping Porsches is a complicated business, and he and his brother try to avoid the Westside whenever possible, preferring to venture to the far reaches of the Valley, where there's much less for the taking. Don't shit where you eat is the logic behind that, but it means long hours of searching for the right car, and then even longer hours casing the car itself. Old, battered air-cooled Porsches may be relatively cheap, but they're never plentiful. And the cars that Tomo prefers to pinch are those with enough visible wear that they aren't likely to attract too much attention from the auto insurer.

As I watch this stoned delinquent playing computer games, I wonder how much longer Tomo can get away with this. By now, someone must have noticed an uptick in stolen Porsche 964s and 993s. Or is nobody watching, nobody keeping score? Is that how life works? We're all just playing pickup?

"Are you ever going to get off that sofa?" I ask.

"What makes you so special?" Tomo says. His eyes are red, bloodshot like the veins of a leaf, and he looks up at me and shakes his head. "Who the fuck are you? If you're a soccer player," he says, pointing to the TV screen, where before there'd been footage of me at my best, "then be a fucking soccer player."

I towel off my hair and then go into the bedroom, sliding on jeans and a blouse, and then I go out and sit down next to Tomo, who's driving his nitrous oxide–modified Porsche 911 Turbo into Las Venturas and attempting to steal a different car from the Italian Mafia.

"Did you ever think about doing anything else?" I ask.

"You mean playing *Warcraft* or something?"

"No, I mean, in life," I say. "Not being, you know, a criminal."

I've never said that before, called him a criminal. He pauses the game, squints at me, picks up the blunt, exhales it in my face. He raises his free hand and holds it next to my face, as if he's going to slap me.

I sit there, blinking, waiting, but he doesn't hit me; instead, he points at my crooked nose.

"Don't fucking judge me," he says. "You haven't done shit either."

He's right. But I've kept in shape. My game is tight. Maybe I can still play? My feet will carry me for a few more seasons. Playing with the boys has helped. It's kept my skills up. My shortcoming is the same one I've always had: to fit into a team, to play with other girls. And Pauline is finally showing signs of being, well, not normal, but more normal, I guess.

"Fuck it," I tell Tomo. "Call Ricky."

—

We send Ricky a dozen copies of the DVD, more highlights from my time with the USWNT, enough copies for him to send them to general managers at women's professional clubs around the world. This was the footage that got me into college, of course, even with my reputation as the biter. You saw that tape, and you took a chance on me, or at least one school did. And it paid off for UC Miramar, as we played for the Division II championships twice during my career. Ricky already has my college tape.

—

We're sitting at a picnic table in the Brentwood Country Mart. I've finished a half chicken from the rotisserie place next to the courtyard, and now I'm twisting my straw around an iced tea. I sit with my chin in my palm, elbow on the plank picnic table. I'm aware I look like a petulant teen, but that's how I feel. Maybe I don't want to play with another women's team. What if I can't? Who is Tomo to be dictating my life choices?

"Maybe you'll get a game," Ricky says. "If you want one. I can reach out to Coach Tony, ask him for a reference."

"He would do that?" I say.

"I think so," he says. "He knows you can play. We can tell him you've matured."

I haven't, have I? But I don't say that.

“Are there other WUSA squads that might, um, bite?” I say. “California squads? San Jose, maybe? I gotta stay close to home.”

Ricky says the only way I’ll get a game is if I’m willing to play overseas. Denmark. Sweden. Maybe Japan.

“So I can only play abroad?” I say.

Ricky nods. “It’s a clearer path.”

I tell him I don’t think I can do that. Because of my family.

Tomo says I’d be a fool not to take an overseas offer. “How cool would that be?” He grins.

Who am I kidding? I can’t go anywhere. I can’t leave Pauline. And I won’t abandon her to another facility.

Chapter 34

I hear her moaning in the front yard, a doleful sound, more cetacean than human, a cry of distress. I run outside, and she's sitting on the lawn, clothes disheveled, hair messed up, makeup even more askew than usual. Her eyes are bulging, her nose is bruised, her lower lip swollen.

She shrieks when I try to hug her, to stand her up. It's as if she's been dropped here, discarded, used up, and I look up and down the street, as if whoever left her might still be walking away. When I help her inside, she starts crying, panicked, as if she's somehow misbehaved.

"You haven't done anything wrong, Paul," I tell her.

"B-b-b-b-bad boy," she says.

"You're a good girl," I tell her. "You're okay."

"He t-t-t-t-ouched me," she says.

"Who?"

"B-b-b-b-bad boy. He touched me."

No. No. What she means is someone pushed her, right? Or maybe stole something from her? Or . . . *No.*

She'd been assaulted during her walk to the village.

I call 911. I don't remove Pauline's pants; I don't shower her. I leave her on the sofa in the den and wait for the police and paramedics.

When they show up, Pauline is agitated, rocking back and forth, shaking her head, stammering, despite the two lorazepam tablets that

I've given her. The pair of male officers say they need to wait for her legal conservator to arrive, and when my father finally pulls up, his "Open House" signs and lawn spears in the back seat of his car, he's prepared. I've already told him over the phone what appears to have happened. His response is to sigh. Finally, Samira, the paramedic, arrives, and I tell her I haven't cleaned Pauline or bathed her, so a rape kit could still be administered.

My father is shaking his head, tearing up, and he retreats through the kitchen to the living room.

Come on, I'm thinking. *Come on, Dad. We need you on this one.*

"Sir, we would like to take your daughter to Saint John's, to the ER," one of the officers says.

"Um, can we do whatever you need to do here?" I ask, turning to my father, who is leaning against the doorframe between the kitchen and the living room, his broad back, clothed in a denim shirt, to us. "Dad?"

He has his face in his hand. "What?"

"We need to take your daughter to the ER," the officer repeats.

"You can talk to her," I tell Samira. "She's right here."

Pauline is rocking back and forth, attempting to block out the crowded room.

"Can you guys wait in, like, outside, or . . . ," I say to the officers.

They look at each other, shake their heads. "We can't leave the crime scene." So that's what this is?

"She was outside when I found her."

"C-c-c-car ride," Pauline suddenly interjects.

"You were in a car?" I ask.

"B-b-b-boyfriend."

"Does she have a boyfriend?" Samira asks me. "Do you have a boyfriend?" she asks Pauline.

Pauline doesn't answer.

"Honey," Samira says. "I'm going to check you, to look at those bruises, to see if you're all right, okay? Can you roll your eyes all the way to your left?"

Pauline doesn't understand the command, but the paramedic seems satisfied with what she's seeing. She shines the light from side to side and then holds up two fingers.

"Follow my fingers."

"Pauline, look at her fingers, okay?" I tell her. "Look while she moves them. Keep looking."

She hasn't been concussed, and the bruising around her nose is determined not to be a serious cause for concern. And her jaw, thank god, appears undamaged.

"Can you stand up? Can you walk?" Samira asks.

Pauline doesn't respond.

"Walk?" Samira says again.

Pauline nods.

"We'll take her," I say. "Dad? Come on. We'll take her to Saint John's."

The paramedic looks at the cops, shrugs. "That's fine with me."

"I have to p-p-pee. I want to clean up."

"No, not if we're doing an SAEK," Samira says.

"What's that?"

"Sexual assault evidence kit."

My father's wandered off.

"Dad? Come on, let's go," I shout.

"Pauline," I tell her. "Just hold off for a few minutes, okay? Till we're at the . . . the doctor's."

Samira says the emergency services technicians will be waiting for us. They'll gather the DNA, the hair, whatever.

I drive. My father sits in the passenger seat. Pauline sits in back and pees in her pants.

She's so brave, holding my hand while a technician swabs her genitals, her soaked underwear, her jeans. They gather a half dozen hairs and what may be semen as I cry.

My father sits in the waiting room, flipping through an issue of *Discover*.

Once the swabbing is finished, the hair samples are taken, and the blood samples drawn, and once they've administered Zithromax and Suprax for possible exposure to sexually transmitted diseases, as well as an emergency contraceptive, I ask for a wet towel, which the nurses say they don't have, instead giving me a white plastic container of wet napkins. I scrub Pauline as best I can, but while I'm wiping her, the stress of the afternoon and evening begin to get to Pauline, and she starts shouting, repeating consonant syllables in a rhythmic hum.

"I'm sorry," I tell her. "I'm so sorry."

She's rocking back and forth again. We've been here for hours. She's been probed. She's been swabbed. She's been examined. Nobody's fed her. It's all my fault. How could I have been so irresponsible?

"We'll get something to eat, Paul, okay?" I take her in my arms, give her a hug, smell her sweaty scalp, her hair, which smells like straw. She's beat up, used up, a girl who can't cope with a damn thing, and now she's being asked to cooperate in her own humiliation.

I'm thinking maybe I should have just taken her home or never agreed to any kind of investigation. Asking her to bear this imposition seems almost as great as the assault itself.

Maybe that's why my father never filed charges against Rod at Found Horizons; maybe he knew how much it would take out of all of us.

"It's almost over," I tell her. "Okay, just hang on. I'm going to find a doctor."

I go to the nurses' station, find the attending physician, a South Asian man with a University of Tennessee button next to his name tag,

Dr. Pappu. I tell him I want to take my sister home, and he says we can't go, not yet, not until a detective arrives to collect the samples and talk to us.

"When will that be?" I ask.

He says, "I'll call them again."

I go out to the waiting room and find my father sitting there, staring up at television footage of Iraq—rough, grainy images of a Humvee apparently running over an IED, flipping onto its side.

"Can you get us some food, get Pauline something?"

"What?"

"Sweet-and-sour pork?" I say.

"Where am I going to find that?" he asks.

"Comfort food, something she likes. She's been through hell."

He looks down at his hands. He has tears in his eyes. Blinking, he looks up, shakes his head. Then stands. "Okay, okay, I'll find something."

A detective named Peggy Cherng, with hair that's sculpted up into a kind of pompadour and then pulled back into a ponytail, arrives. "Excuse me," she says, and then removes the gum she's been chewing, folding it into a yellow Post-it she then tosses into the orange plastic bin with the jagged "Biohazardous Waste" sign on it.

"Okay," she says, looking down at a clipboard. She repeats Pauline's name and then asks for her legal conservator, my father, who isn't present. She shakes her head. "Gotta wait for him."

As we wait, I ask her what the next steps will be. She tells me we'll have to wait for the lab results, and then, based on those, her department might open an investigation.

"Can you . . . ," she says to Pauline, who is rocking back and forth. Then she turns to me. "Can she, when the time comes, when your father is here, tell us what happened?"

I look at Pauline, who is now nodding her head. She's hungry. She wants to go home.

My father returns with some orange chicken in goopy sauce and some white rice, which we spill onto a paper plate for Pauline, and she eats with her fingers. I don't bother to correct her or urge her to use her fork. She's hungry; I let her eat.

I pet her on the head. "Hey, baby."

She blinks, leans her head into my hand. Her face is so beautiful, angelic even, our mother's Italianate features so pronounced and lovely. She could have modeled if she were taller, if she could follow directions, if she were a completely different person. In reality, her face hasn't been any more than a curse.

No, that's an awful way to look at it. She's been betrayed by whoever did this to her.

"I'm s-s-sorry," she says.

"You did nothing wrong, Paul. You're an angel. It's the world that's so awful."

She chews her food, the starchy sauce squishing out of the side of her mouth, and I wipe it away.

When we're finally home, my father pours himself a 7 and 7 and then sits down on a dining chair he's brought into the den. He takes a sip and says to Pauline, who's sitting on the sofa, her legs folded beneath her, head in my lap, "So what happened?"

She shakes her head. She's embarrassed, apparently, unwilling to admit what's happened.

"Dad," I tell him. "Let me."

He shakes his head, takes another sip. He's heartbroken. He feels helpless. A father wants to protect his daughter, and this—this must feel like the greatest failure of all.

"I'm so sorry, Paul," he says, tears welling up again. "I don't know how to fix this."

There's no fixing this, of course; there's only trying to get through it. I pet Pauline's head, smoothing down her hair, watching her close her eyes. Dad goes into his room, puts on his relaxing tape, the soothing baritone voice urging him to feel his fingers going limp, to feel his hands settling, to feel his arms relaxing, to feel the energy leaving his body. He plays dead.

I take Pauline into the bathroom, run the bath, squeeze in some bath gel, tell her to take off her clothes. She's reluctant, but she slowly strips. She's so pale that in the tub, her hair appears inky black, as if it were squirted from a squid. Amid a mountainous archipelago of bubbles, she seems as if she's starting to feel like herself again, playing gingerly with the suds. I run a washcloth over her face, careful of where she is bruised.

"Paul," I say. "Can you tell me who did this?"

She shakes her head. "B-b-bad boy."

"But who? Who did this to you?"

"B-b-boyfriend."

"My boyfriend? Tomo?" I say, my heart cracking.

She shakes her head. "Old b-b-boyfriend."

I'm trying to figure out who she might mean. She never met any of my college flings, short-lived as they were. And from high school, the only person who might possibly fit that description is—

"Brendan?"

She nods.

"Are you sure? Brendan. Tall? From high school?"

"B-b-b-brendan," she says. "B-b-bad boy."

I've never known Pauline to lie. "Are you sure?" I ask her.

She ignores me, squeezing the washcloth under the water and watching air bubbles surface.

"Paul," I say, "are you—"

She looks up at me. "Yes."

I call Tomo that night.

When he comes over, we sit in the front yard, not far from where I found Pauline this afternoon.

I tell him what's happened, how I don't know what I should do. I'm struggling to get it all out, blubbering some of the words, having to backtrack to make myself understandable. Tomo doesn't interrupt.

He asks me simple questions. Who is the guy? Why didn't I tell him before that Brendan had gotten forceful with me? Where does he live?

He stands up, brushes himself off, and rubs something invisible from his scalp with his hand. He gives me a hug. I breathe in his breath and feel myself inflate. I'm still strong. Nothing fucking knocks me down. But then, just an instant after he's gone, when I'm back inside, I deflate.

Chapter 35

I can't fix Pauline. I can't fix my father. I can't fix myself. I can't sleep anymore. I can't unclench my muscles until I see the results of the SAEK. I keep running through all the mistakes I think I've made—I never should have taught Pauline to wear makeup; I never should have blown out her hair; I never should have allowed her to walk by herself to the village, a half mile that seemed so safe. I sit up in bed, in the still-dark predawn, tie on a pair of Asics, and head off on a five-mile run, from our house to the beach, up the trail to the cliffs, and then up the long, last half-mile grade to our house—the route Pauline took. The first sprinklers swish on in the murk, the last coyotes scissoring back to their dens, and another day dawns in everyone's fucking normal life.

As I run, I picture Brendan's narrow face, his thick eyebrows, his blue eyes, the whole long, angular, symmetrical horror of him. It is stubbornly visible in front of me, a hologram taunting me through the morning fog, and when I get home, I call Tomo. He doesn't pick up. He's been scarce since that night, and I don't blame him. I never told him about Brendan, and I never told him about the night I'd gone home with him.

Pauline is awake. She's now afraid to leave the house; she stays in her room or in the den, assorting her makeup into piles, shaking her head when I ask whether she wants to go get some lunch. I heat up toast and butter it, and she chews quickly before returning to her assortment.

I've asked her a dozen times. "Are you sure it was Brendan? Are you absolutely sure?"

Sometimes she nods. Sometimes she says yes.

Detective Cherng comes over to discuss the case with us. There's enough DNA evidence to prosecute, but she's not sure she can get a warrant to collect a sample from the accused to see whether there's a match.

"ASD testimony is—well, the district attorney says it's not an easy path."

She says that even if they find corroborating DNA evidence, Brendan can still easily claim the sex was consensual.

She's sitting on a kitchen chair we've moved into the den. Pauline sits beside me, holding my hand. Her fingernails need trimming.

"Pauline," Detective Cherng says. "Can you tell me what happened that afternoon? Can you tell me in order, from the very beginning?"

Pauline is rocking slightly. "I w-w-w-went to get ice cream."

"She was walking," I say.

Detective Cherng looks at me to silence me. "What time did you leave?"

Pauline can't answer this. She's never had any sense of time. "I w-w-was walking."

"I know, but what time did you leave?"

Detective Cherng looks down at her notepad. She's written three lines. "Pauline, you're going to have to give me the whole day. Everything that happened, in order. Can you do that?"

Pauline doesn't respond.

My father, standing with a cup of coffee in his hand, slams his fist against the wall. Detective Cherng turns to him. "Would it be okay with you, and with you, if I talk to Pauline alone?"

We both agree and retreat to the living room.

A half hour later, Detective Cherng comes out, sliding her notepad into her back pocket. She exhales sharply. "Nothing easy about this."

I think that's something of an understatement, but I shrug.

"She's clear about who did this. I will say that," Detective Cherng says. "But can I get a timeline out of her?" She shakes her head. "I don't know. I don't know if the DA will want to try this. I can't even say a judge will issue a warrant."

"But the rape kit, you said, showed some trauma," I said.

"That's consistent with sexual assault, yes," Detective Cherng said. "Also consistent with rough intercourse. I, I'm sorry, but I'm just spelling everything out."

My father nods.

"Can she do a Q&A? That's all the DA wants to know. He doesn't want to bring a case that will lower his batting average."

"What are you saying?"

She shrugs. "I'll be in touch."

"About the statement? The warrant?" I ask.

"Sure, all of that."

Pauline doesn't want to talk about any of it. When I bring it up, she gives me a strange sort of smile and bobs her head, acknowledging me and the subject but not offering any more about it.

She's sure it was Brendan. Remembers him vividly from high school. And when I ask whether she could point him out, could tell the story to strangers, she makes that same smiling and bobbing gesture.

"Look," my father says to me when we're alone in the kitchen. "Maybe we let it go. Maybe it's not something she's up to, that we're up to."

"I'm up to it," I say.

"I know that," he says, but then adds, "but you're not Pauline."

Detective Cherng swears she wants to bring charges, but in two attempts to get a statement, once here at the house and once in Van Nuys at the county courthouse, Pauline has failed to provide a timeline that seems credible and is repeatable, by her, in court.

But Detective Cherng has convinced the DA to ask a judge to issue a warrant to procure Brendan's DNA.

When she calls with that news, I'm thinking *we have him; we fucking have him.* We're going to at least get the satisfaction of justice.

But no, there's still the problem of Pauline's testimony being reliable, of her being able to repeat any statement in open court. The accused has a right to confront his accuser in court, even if she's profoundly autistic.

"So that's it?" I ask Detective Cherng. "When a special-needs kid gets assaulted, there's no crime, no arrest?"

"She's not a kid," Detective Cherng says. "She's above the age of consent. How can we win this thing? That's what the DA will ask me."

How can I go abroad to play soccer, to try out for a team in Norway or Japan, while my sister is going through this? I go through my days as a zombie, showing up at Hops; taking the orders; delivering cocktails, tempura tacos, jalapeño yellowtail. The bar clientele is rapidly changing, and Fernando is talking about opening the upstairs, the card room, using the space for more dinner traffic. That would mean throwing the guys out, ending the decades-long tradition of card games, but most of the men have aged out of heavy drinking and nightly card playing. The fisherman with the cat who follows him around hasn't shown up in months. Lost at sea for all we know.

My father says he's unable to concentrate on his card games, doesn't bother to read tip sheets for his weekly bets. He's down to hustling rentals at the real estate firm, while the rest of the brokers are getting rich in a booming real estate market. Our town has been discovered, and now waves of buyers are coming in and tearing down houses and putting up

McMansions, and these folks don't want to buy from a middle-aged guy with a shaggy beard in a corduroy jacket and captain's hat. They're buying from women with blond tips, leather-interior SUVs, tight stretchy pants, and calf-high boots.

My dad doesn't stand a chance.

And the card room is anachronistic in a town increasingly devoted to prosperous families. Where will he go then? Will he just retire into his room and listen to his relaxation tape?

Is that my future?

I gather my boots and my kit and drive out to Fairfax to play in a pickup game with some Israelis and Salvadorans. It's a nasty game, full of hard tackles on a pitch that's more dirt than grass, under hot late-afternoon Hollywood sun, with unforgiving players who exploit opponents' mistakes like cheetahs picking off the weakest in a herd. I'm playing in front, and in the first fifteen minutes of the match, I've made a half dozen slide tackles, and an Israeli player in a white shirt and yarmulke has to be restrained from attacking me.

I stand my ground, glare at him, because I'm thinking, *Come on, please. Try me. Hurt me.* But the game is still there for me.

And I want to see Tomo, but he's not returning my texts or calls.

Chapter 36

Finally, Detective Cherng tells us she's secured a search warrant from a judge to take a sample of Brendan's DNA. Brendan appears at the courthouse crime lab to provide blood and hair samples that determine that he's a match, that his semen was indeed in my sister, and now, we are sure, it's a matter of time before he'll be arrested.

I sit down with Pauline and talk to her about the case, her story, about how she first met Brendan when I was in high school, about how she saw him again when she was walking to get frozen yogurt. He was driving his car? What kind of car? Did he offer you a ride? Did he tell you to get in? When did he touch you? How? Where?

She freezes up, can't continue the Q&A, and after a few minutes, I have to give up the inquisition. I lose my patience with her, shaking my head, cursing under my breath, because all she has to do is tell the damn story the same way, on repeat, and all the rest of her life is on some kind of repeat, so why isn't this?

But even with Detective Cherng, and then a young lawyer from the district attorney's office, May Lee, coming to help with the coaching, every time we try, Pauline has to start from scratch, has to be reminded who Detective Cherng is, why she is here, what Brendan did, when he did it.

I can see the impatience on the detective's face, the disappointment of the attorney, who has apparently coached dozens of rape victims but never one quite as inarticulate as this one.

"Don't give up," I plead with them as May Lee fills her roller suitcase with her notes, saying she's already late for her next appointment back at the office.

"Usually," she says, almost in passing, "the victims come downtown, and we take the statements there. Let's try that, okay? Next time." Turning her attention to Pauline, she says, "Maybe the change in scenery will cause you to focus."

Pauline doesn't listen.

"Sure," I answer for her.

I dress her in black slacks, a white blouse. She becomes pouty when I refuse to put a heavy coat of makeup on her face. I don't want her looking like some femme fatale for this visit to the district attorney's office; I just want her looking like any other young girl. She's still pretty with just a touch of eyeliner, a little blush, and lipstick. I sit in the driver's seat, my dad next to me, and Pauline sits in the back seat of the Volvo. She's smiling, mumbling a little rhyme that she's taken to saying: "Trudy, Daddy, Paulie, makes three. Trudy, Daddy, Paulie . . ." She becomes agitated when we hit a patch of traffic on Sunset, starts rocking, but I calm her down by handing her a Starburst candy.

When we arrive downtown, we wait in a third-floor anteroom, a linoleum-floored space with a portrait of Governor Schwarzenegger framed above a naïve, rough version of the great seal of California—the goddess Minerva, the shield, the bear eating grapes—that is painted directly onto the wall. There's a potted plant that at first looks real, but after sitting and waiting in front of the clear Plexiglas window for about ten minutes, I realize it's fake.

Finally, a heavy wooden door with a rectangular window about head high opens, and May Lee comes out and says we should follow her.

But instead of going into an interview room to do a statement, she takes us down to Detective Cherng's office, which is across the courtyard, in another building, where dozens of people seem to be waiting on metal benches lining the walls.

We're buzzed into a room with a mirror on one side and told to take seats, and when I ask May why we are doing the statement here, she tells me to wait a moment and returns with Detective Cherng.

She comes in with two bottles of water, handing one to my sister and one to me—I guess I'm supposed to share it with my father.

"I'm surprised you showed up," she says.

"Why?"

"With Brendan being, you know, deceased."

I look at Pauline, then back at Detective Cherng. "What?"

"Discovered yesterday afternoon in his mobile home by a neighbor, some blunt-force wounds to the head. His place was burgled, valuables missing, apparently a home invasion."

My father, seated next to me, starts to say, "Wait, I'm confused. You mean to say—"

I turn to him and say, "Brendan is dead."

He shakes his head. "Holy shit."

"Yeah," Detective Cherng says. She's looking from me to my father, taking in our facial expressions, attempting to read, I suppose, any sign that we're somehow involved in what can't be a simple coincidence.

I reach down and scratch my arm even though it is not itchy. "So I guess there's no need for a statement," I say.

Pauline's been listening, and now she rocks slightly back and forth, obviously relieved at not having to perform this afternoon.

"May I ask you a few questions?" Detective Cherng says. "Both of you?"

My father looks at me, and then back at Detective Cherng. “Should we have a lawyer present?”

I shake my head. “I’m not worried. Fine. Go ahead.”

She asks where we were yesterday. I was at work. My father was home with Pauline.

Before that I was home with Pauline. My father was in his office at the real estate agency. Our day is fully accounted for, every single minute.

“I didn’t fucking kill Brendan,” I say when I’m asked to repeat my whereabouts. “I should have. But I didn’t, okay?”

She says she’ll be in touch.

Chapter 37

I call Tomo. I text him. Nothing. He's a ghost.

But I talk to Ricky a few days later. The Lady Antlers, a team in Kawasaki, a city south of Tokyo, are interested in signing me. The coach remembers me from the Three Nations tournament, when I put in that brace against Japan in the consolation game. In fact, Japanese national team coaches and players had been wondering for the last seven years what had happened to me. I buried them in the third-place game, and they assumed they would see more of me at the 1999 World Cup, but instead, I'd disappeared from international soccer.

They'll fly me over and put me on a ten-game contract, and if I stick, they'll sign me for the season. Right now, the offer is a plane ticket, twenty nights in a hotel, and about $5,000 in game checks, and that's all. But a single-season contract would pay me something like $70,000 for playing soccer.

"This is your shot," Ricky says.

But it doesn't feel like it. It feels like I'm abandoning my father, my sister. If I go, Pauline goes back into an assisted-living facility or a state institution. I'm sure of it.

When I tell my father, he says, "You have to go, True. You've gotta." But I can't. I tell Ricky I'll think about it, but I know I can't leave my family.

—

Pauline is too frightened to leave the house, barely leaves her room or the dining room, arranging her makeup—her pencils and liners, her compacts. It relaxes her, I realize, like a kind of rosary, and I suppose that watching her calm herself is my own form of meditation. While I sit with her, I know that nothing bad is happening to her. I must keep her safe. How can I leave her?

My father says that he can manage. But how? He doesn't have anything saved, and caring for Pauline is expensive. How can he afford to hire a full-time caregiver while he goes out and tries to hustle a condominium? He can't do it. We don't have the money. She'll have to go back into an institution.

"Don't think about us," he urges me.

But I do. I have to. I've spent my life thinking about us. *Trudy, Daddy, Paulie makes three . . .*

"Are you going to p-p-play?" Pauline asks me, shoving a handful of white rice into her mouth. "P-p-play soccer?"

My only thought is that I need a good run. On a real pitch. Everything in my life turns to shit except one thing, and that one thing is a soccer ball.

But that night, while Pauline and I are assorting her makeup into categories—eyes, lips, skin—one of her favorite activities, I say, "What if I go play soccer in, like, Germany?"

She's not paying attention.

Eyes. Eyes. Eyes. She's laying eyebrow brushes next to each other.

"Paul," I say. "I may have a chance to go play in another country, far away." She still doesn't lift her head to look at me.

"Paul—"

She stops sorting the pencils. "Y-y-y-you have to go, okay? You have to."

Chapter 38

2005

I'm living in what the Japanese call a 1LDK. It's a six-tatami-mat living room with a convenience kitchen, a similarly tiny bedroom, and a bathroom with plastic walls. I wake up early, eat a chicken breast, drink some milk, grab my kit, and head to the practice facility, a soccer pitch that's the infield grass of Tamagawa University's track-and-field facility. The Kawasaki Lady Antlers, it turns out, don't have their own practice facility, and two days a week we have to make do with this college pitch. We're allowed to use the facilities of Kawasaki Frontale, the local men's J1 League team, on other afternoons, though when our seasons overlap—the start of our season coincides with the conclusion of the men's—we're reduced to the college pitch and its concrete locker room, which on cold winter afternoons is freezing.

But the practices and games are fierce. I'm one of two foreign players on the roster, and I live in the same building as Ula, a nineteen-year-old Swedish player who spends all her time off the pitch speaking to her parents back in Gothenburg. We share a taxi to Tamagawa University, and while I try to reassure her that she's doing fine, that she's playing well, that she's getting the hang of the 4-3-3 Ota Sensei has us playing, I know that she'll be gone in a few weeks. She doesn't have the toughness to make it over here, on the other side of the world, far from her home and away from her friends and Swedish teammates. She's on loan from her Swedish club, and she has yet to see any game time.

I was inserted into the starting lineup my second game in a Kawasaki Lady Antlers purple-and-gold strip, and I scored my first goal in the eighty-eighth minute, a volley on a good cross from a Japanese forward named Egawa with whom I'd already formed an on-pitch bond that had us each looking for the other as soon as we were on the ball.

Egawa has made my adjustment to the team seamless, making it clear to her teammates that she feels I can help us win games. Ota Sensei, a corpulent man with a pockmarked face who's always looking down at his clipboard and frowning, is the kind of coach who devotes himself to studying our opponents more than running our practices. He leaves Egawa to run those, and she runs us through several kilometers of fitness before each day's scrimmages, and I've made it a point, after the first week of getting my wind back, to finish at the top of my group. The scrimmages, in the hard January rain, with wind that devils high balls, remind me of what I've been missing. And the games themselves are blissful gaps in my life where I feel totally and completely myself. Here, on these Japanese pitches, in Yokohama, Tokyo, Nagoya, and Hiroshima, playing with Japanese women to crowds of young Japanese girls waving their little flags and eating dried squid on sticks, I've finally found where I belong.

In the evenings, after home games, I meet up with Tomo, and we walk along the shopping street near my apartment, or up on the cliffs over Yokohama Bay, where there are bakeries and Japanese families having cake and coffee, and he asks me how I feel about my sister, about my father, and I tell him I feel awful because I've never felt so free.

And I don't ask about Brendan.

All I know is that Tomo flew to Japan a day after Brendan was killed.

In the evenings after practices, Tomo stays over at my little apartment. We have a dinner of yakitori or soba, and we lie down on my futon and we talk only about tomorrow, my next game. When Tomo tries to engage me in a longer-term plan, I don't respond. I shut down. I don't talk about my father. I pretend I have forgotten about Pauline. I tell him I need to focus on the pitch.

But sometimes, during practice, during the last scrimmage of the day, I'll stop running and walk, just watching the ball. For a moment, I can hear Pauline, her stutter. She's saying my name. The game moves past me, to the other end of the pitch, and I'm just standing there. I look like this: _______I_______ and Egawa will shout at me to run.

So I go.

Epilogue

2017

I ended up playing professionally in four countries: Japan, Denmark, France, and finally Sweden. I scored 186 game goals in a 348-game professional soccer career, had nearly as many assists, and ended up winning two club championships. I was named the Japan Women's Football League Most Valuable Player of 2007. However, I never did play for the United States Women's National Team again.

Tomo was arrested in 2006 in connection with a stolen car ring in Kawasaki. He is spending fifteen years in Kofu Prison. I visited him three times. Then I found him to be a distraction. Soccer must always come first. That's how I survive. When I moved from Japan to Denmark, to join FC Fyn, I wrote to tell him about the transfer. We haven't spoken in eight years.

I haven't talked to my father or Pauline in twelve years.

For my last season, I played in the Swedish Second Division: cold, hard pitches in windy, half-empty stadiums. Stout Nordic defenders with legs like tree trunks who played in single-digit Celsius temperatures in short sleeves. We won our division and a spot in the UEFA Women's Champions League. Our second group-stage game was against a French First Division club.

Mother Time is undefeated. She will beat the best players in the world. She will even make the girl on the cover of *Time* in her sports bra when she was twenty a little less lovely.

Alexis was another thirty-seven-year-old winding down her career playing wherever she could get a game and a paycheck. She was a midfielder for Nantes, our group-stage opponent.

It was the first time we had been on the same pitch in twenty years.

Her warm-ups, her sideways lunging runs and crossover scissors, her hopping up and down on her toes, even the way her ponytail bounced, were as familiar to me as the creases on my own palms, despite the years.

She nodded to me before the game, came over to shake my hand.

I turned away from her. Then we kicked off, and I could sense immediately she had lost her first step, that her damaged knees had finally betrayed her, were no longer the lethal instruments they had been. Now, she gave away her intended direction by a shift of her weight, a tilting of her shoulder, a gathering of energy before she touched the ball.

I skinned her with an easy feint left, then a touch right, and was gone.

She could not stay with me.

I put in two goals in the first twenty-two minutes.

After her coach benched her, I lost interest in the match. The player who was brought on, a Senegalese with powerful thighs and calves and a game built more on speed and strength than talent and guile, had obviously been told by her coach to mark me.

She shadowed me everywhere I went, and I began to sit deep in the midfield, helping our defense preserve our two-goal lead.

But Alexis knew, and I knew: I had fucking destroyed her.

Those first years in Japan, I could still hear Pauline's voice, her stuttering start to words, her repetition of meaningless syllables. It was as if she were in the next room. A mumble coming through the walls. Then, after a season, she spoke to me less often.

By the time I transferred to FC Fyn in Denmark's Elitedivisionen, I could remember her voice, but I seldom heard her.

And now, my professional career over, I'm running on a sand pitch, playing a pickup game on a beach with palm trees for goals on an island in the Gulf of Siam against Israeli ex-army men and British boys on their gap year. I'm the only girl. I can barely hear my sister at all.

But then there she is: *T-t-t-true.*

And I run to open space.

ACKNOWLEDGMENTS

- Becky Sweren
- Vivian Lee
- David Kuhn
- George Quraishi
- Barry Harbaugh
- David Hirshey
- Nick McDonell
- Ptolemy Tompkins
- Josh Greenfeld
- Silke, Esmee, and Lola

ABOUT THE AUTHOR

New York Times bestselling author Karl Taro Greenfeld penned the novels *The Subprimes* and *Triburbia*, a *New York Times* Editor's Choice. His memoir, *Boy Alone*, was a *Washington Post* Best Book of the Year. Karl has also written *Dr. J: The Autobiography* (coauthored with Julius Erving), *NowTrends*, *China Syndrome*, *Standard Deviations*, and *Speed Tribes*. His prizewinning writing has appeared in *Harper's Magazine*, the *Atlantic*, the *Paris Review*, *Vogue*, *GQ*, the *New York Times*, and others. His books have been translated into twelve languages.

Karl currently lives in California with his wife and two daughters—both of whom played youth soccer with neither distinction nor enthusiasm.